RIPPLES ON THE WATER

How to Cultivate the Servant's Spirit

Books By Judy Miller

    Cups Running Over
    Seasons of the Heart
    Seasons of Celebration
    It Only Takes a Spark
    Hold Gently This Bright Hour
    New Day Dawning
    Heart Against a Thorn
    Ripples on the Water

RIPPLES
ON THE
WATER

How to Cultivate the Servant's Spirit

By Judy Miller

Dawn Publications
2103 N. Memorial Ct.
Pasadena, Texas 77502

Ripples On The Water
  How To Cultivate The Servant's Spirit
Copyright 1990 by Judy Miller
ISBN: 0-942341-04-X

All rights reserved. No part of this publication may be reproduced, stored in a retrieval system, or transmitted in any form or by any means — electronic, mechanical, photocopy, recording, or any other — except for brief quotations in printed reviews without the prior permission of the author.

Printed in the United States of America.

CONTENTS

Foreword by Fairy Parker
Preface
Introduction
1. Servanthood Defined . . . . Page 17
2. Serving God in the Spirit . . . . Page 25
3. A Willing Spirit . . . . Page 37
4. An Unselfish Spirit . . . . Page 49
5. A Sacrificial Spirit . . . . Page 63
6. A Cooperative Spirit . . . . Page 79
7. A Devotional Spirit . . . . Page 95
8. A Humble Spirit . . . . Page 111
9. A Winsome Spirit . . . . Page 123
10. A Neighborly Spirit . . . . Page 135
11. A Home-Loving Spirit . . . . Page 149
12. A Joyful Spirit . . . . Page 159
13. A Loving, Compassionate Spirit . . . . Page 169

ACKNOWLEDGMENTS

For the most part, all Scriptures unless otherwise indicated are taken from the New King James Version (NKJV). Copyright 1979, 1980, 1982. Thomas Nelson Inc., Publishers.

Scripture taken from the Holy Bible: New International Version. Copyright 1978 by the International Bible Society.

Grateful appreciation to the following for permission to include in this book the following selections:

Shannon Caldwell, *A Woman's Spirit Of Service*. Used by permission.

Lloyd C. Douglas, *Magnificent Obsession*. Willet, Clark and Company, Chicago: 440 South Dearborn Street, New York, N.Y. 200 Fifth Avenue.

Richard J. Foster, *Celebration of Discipline*. Published by Harper and Row, Publishers, Inc., 10 East 53rd Street, New York, N.Y. 10022. Copyright 1978.

John Gibson, *You Can't Strut Before God*. Excerpt from THE KEY-NOTER, bulletin of the Sixth and Izard Church of Christ, Little Rock, Arkansas. Used by permission.

Joyce Girourd, "How Would It Be?" Used by permission.

Helen Keller, *The Story of My Life*. Published by Doubleday and Company, Inc., Garden City, New York, 1954.

Madeline L'Engle, *Walking On Water: Reflections on Faith and Art*. Wheaton, Ill. Harold Shaw Publishers, 1972. p. 122.

Max Lucado, from the book *God Came Near*. Copyright 1987 by Max Lucado. Published by Multnomah Press, Portland, Oregon 97266. Used by permission.

Mary Morrone, *A Lesson in Giving*. Excerpt from SUNSHINE magazine, Litchfield, Illinois 62056. Used by permission.

Mary Oler, "Who Is My Neighbor?" Used by permission.

Harvey Porter, Excerpt from bulletin article. Used by permission.

Garnett Ann Schultz, "The Seeds We Sow," from *Where There Is Love*. Published by Harlo Press. "I Planted A Garden," from *But Not My Heart*. Published by Dorrance And Company. Copyright 1969. Used by permission.

Mary Welch, *Reckoning At Dusk*. Published by Macalester Park Publishing Company. 1571 Grand Avenue, Saint Paul, Minnesota. 1953.

Many thanks and appreciation to Fairy Parker of the Southeast Church of Christ in Houston, Texas for an excellent job of editing this manuscript, and for writing the Foreword.

During the time I was writing this book, my greatest encouragement came from my dear husband, Jule. I will never be able to tell him how much I appreciate his suggestions, corrections and unfailing support and love.

FOREWORD

This foreword is intended to *fore-warn* all who study this book. It is a warning that you will become a better person, a better citizen of our great nation and a better citizen of God's Kingdom!

No one is better qualified to inspire her readers than Judy Miller. I have known her for many years and have seen her words put into actions. She is truly my idea of an Ideal Christian Woman.

All of our feeble efforts are only as "Ripples on the Water," but this book will teach us to learn "How to Cultivate the Servant's Spirit."

— Farris (Fairy) Parker

PREFACE

Water is vital to mankind. Of all God's natural resources, none is more important than water. The peoples of this earth could not exist without it. Like a tree planted by the rivers of water we are completely dependent upon our earth's water supplies.

Water drops from the sky as rain, but how did it get there? Almost immediately after a rainfall, water begins to evaporate into the air as water vapor. We do not generally observe water vapor but it is all around us.

Water evaporates from the streams, ponds, rivers, lakes and oceans — anything that is wet. The vapor rises because of warm air. The warm air becomes cool, causing tiny drops of water to form. When the drops become too heavy to hang in the atmosphere they begin to fall from the sky. Water that once was evaporated from the earth's wet surfaces has returned to the earth again as rain.

This is a wonderful phenomenon. In God's water cycle, water falls on the earth, returns to the sky, then eventually comes back to the earth. This concept of give and return is a beautiful one. It is a "touch of wonder."

Eventually all the water returns to the seas, but on its route there, it blesses all mankind. Even before these principles were discovered and scientifically explained, the water cycle was described in the Bible:

> All the rivers run into the sea,
> Yet the sea is not full;
> To the place from which the rivers come,
> There they return again (Ecclesiastes 1:7).

Within every person is an endless life stream which, like the water cycle, is renewed time and again. God has placed within the spirit of every Christian "a fountain of water springing up into everlasting life" (John 4:14).

The Christian life is an overflow life. We give from an abundance we have received. As we cast our bread upon the waters (like the water cycle) it always returns to us. Jesus, Himself, teaches us the principle of giving and receiving:

> Give, and it will be given to you: good measure, pressed down, shaken together, and running over will be put into your bosom. For with the same

measure that you use, it will be measured back to you (Luke 6:38).

It is an incredible wonder to be God's servant . . . to be channels of blessings through which His love may flow.

INTRODUCTION

Every Day God calls us to service.
Every Day we respond.

We respond in one of two ways . . . by serving self or others. As followers of Jesus Christ we must, like Paul learn what it means to have "the mind of Christ." Our Lord set the greatest example when He said:

"Yet I am among you as the One who serves" (Luke 22:27).

We are living in a day and age when self fulfillment, self exultation and humanism is not only encouraged but exploited. The "me" generation is "in."

Yet, somewhere along the path between childhood and adulthood, we as Christian women discover that service is our highest calling, our primary fulfillment. Christ has taught us through His word that losing our lives helps us to find them (Matthew 10:39).

As women, God has given us the glorious potential of influence. Serving as wives, mothers, friends, sisters and neighbors enables us to be blessings. As we grow in Christ, certain attributes such as charm, beauty, affection and tenderness are added to our personalities.

We long, like Christ, to possess a sweetness of spirit, warmth of nature and gentleness of character which has been borrowed from Him. These attributes endowed by a loving heavenly Father impart strength, encouragement and comfort to others.

Contrary to popular opinion there are untold opportunities in the church to serve Him. A Christian woman's influence is far reaching.

My Influence

My life shall touch a dozen lives
   before this day is done.
Leave countless marks for good or
   ill ere sets the evening sun,
This is the wish I always wish,
   the prayer I always pray;
Lord, may my life help other lives
   it touches by the way.

— Author Unknown

This book is designed to be used either as a personal study, or a group study in Ladies' Bible classes, neighborhood Bible classes or as research material for retreats or workshops.

Throughout this study we will be learning how to cultivate the servant's spirit.

Cultivation is a beautiful word. The act of cultivating reminds us of a lovely, well-tended garden where graceful flowers and plants are coming to life — blooming and growing.

What happens in the process of cultivation? The first thing which takes place is the weeding out of bad things growing there. Following this, we must dig, plant and work at growing a new and beautiful harvest.

Cultivation of the spirit is a similar process, but the wonderful results are worth the effort.

Service does not come naturally. It is a learning process. There is nothing automatic about it. A child comes into the world with the "me" complex. Every baby has to be taught to be unselfish and to think of the needs of others.

Ecclesiastes 11:1-3; and 6, are wonderful verses for us to contemplate as we begin our study:

> Cast your bread upon the waters,
> For you will find it after many days.
> Give a serving to seven, and also to eight,
> For you do not know what evil will be on the earth.
>
> If the clouds are full of rain,
> They empty themselves upon the earth . . .
> In the morning sow your seed,
> And in the evening do not withhold your hand;

Let this be our mutual prayer, as we seek to cultivate the servant's spirit:

> O Father, help us to cast our bread upon the waters in the form and design of loving acts and gestures of caring. Life will never be long enough to show all the love you have given into our keeping. Help us to share it today. In Jesus Name, Amen.

Drop A Stone

Drop a stone into the water
In a moment it is gone,
But there are a hundred ripples
Circling on and on and on.

Say an unkind word this moment
In a moment it is gone,
But there are a hundred ripples
Circling on and on and on.

Say a word of cheer and splendor
In a moment it is gone,
But there are a hundred ripples
Circling on and on and on.

— Author Unknown

'The generous soul will be made rich,
And he who waters will also be watered himself
(Proverbs 11:25).

CHAPTER ONE

SERVANTHOOD DEFINED

What Does It Mean to Be a Servant?

Paul called himself "a servant of God" on many occasions and in many of his letters. He was very submissive to the will of God. In his epistle to the church at Rome, he described himself in this manner:

> Paul, a servant of Jesus Christ, called to be an apostle, separated to the gospel of God (Romans 1:1).

As he saluted the church at Philippi, he made it clear that he and Timothy were "servants of Jesus Christ" (Philippians 1:1).

Peter also declared himself "a servant and apostle of Jesus Christ" (2 Peter 1:1). James began his book with the same terminology Paul and Peter used.

When we read the letters from these three great servants, we see the urgency in their salutations. These men stated that they were apostles, yet the emphasis seemed to be placed on servanthood.

The term "servant" is not so much a title as a description. Paul, Peter and James were compelled to servanthood.

Doulous

The Greek word for "servant" is *doulous* which means bond-slave or bond-servant. A slave was in bondage to his master; owned by him and gave complete homage to him. He was to obey him always and serve him only. Lynn Anderson, preaching on servanthood, said:

> You cannot be called a "holy," "reverend," "doctor" slave . . . a "right reverend," "master" foot-

washer. If you want to be a servant leader, choose to serve. The one that has the most degrees is not the greatest . . . the one who is *slave* is the greatest.

"But he who is greatest among you shall be your servant (doulous) (Matthew 23:11).

Your Servant, God

God, I worship You today
I give myself to You
As You have given me myself
And all that I may do.

My heart and body, mind and soul
And all I think and say
Are only possible, O God
According to Your way.

And now I give them back to You
As humbly as I can
As much as I may honor You
And serve my fellowman.

I am Your servant and Your slave
Wherever it may be,
And as You made me, I am Yours
For all eternity.

Give me Your love and lasting grace
On every hill and shore
O God, forgive me for my sins
I ask for nothing more.

— Author Unknown.

As transgressors, we once served sin as fervently as any sinner. We obeyed the compulsion to sin as outrageously as any derelict. Chained to its attractions and false allurements our master, Satan, enticed us successfully. He held us, binding us to iniquity until Christ loosed and set us free. Something enormously important happened then:

> But now having been set free from sin, and having become slaves of God, you have your fruit to holiness, and the end, everlasting life (Romans 6:22).

Free at last to serve God from the heart!

> Stand fast therefore in the liberty by which Christ has made us free, and do not be entangled again with a yoke of bondage (Galatians 5:1).

> For you, brethren, have been called to liberty: only do not use liberty as an opportunity for the flesh, but through love serve one another (Galatians 5:13).

Diakonos

Another term for "servant" is *diakonos* which is synonymous in the New Testament with the words deacon and minister. The word "service" is rendered *diakonia* which means the same as ministering.

> For those who have served well as deacons obtain for themselves a good standing and great boldness in the faith which is in Christ Jesus (1 Timothy 3:13).

Paul inspired Timothy with these words:

> If you instruct the brethren in these things, you will be a good minister of Jesus Christ, nourished in the words of faith and of the good doctrine which you have carefully followed (1 Timothy 4:6).

What an encouragement Paul was to Timothy.

Why is it that when we hear the term "minister" we think of only one person — the preacher? It is true that elders, deacons and preachers should demonstrate the highest form of service. In fact, when leaders are not willing to live the life of a servant, they are not worthy of these offices. These positions designate the humblest aspects of servanthood. A minister deacon or elder who only desires leadership, never servanthood, is living a lie. He is modeling his life not after Christ but after his own ego.

Sundoulos

There is another Greek term which is interesting and quite beautiful. The term *sundoulos* means "fellow servant." We are all servants of the living God — therefore we share a fellowship of serving.

In the book of Colossians, we read about Epaphras and Tychicus who are called dear faithful ministers (diakonos) and fellow servants (sundoulos) in the Lord. We have a sundoulos relationship with God and with one another. We do not serve God alone — we serve God together.

Look at the affectionate way Paul speaks of Epaphras in Colossians 1:7:

> . . . as you also learned from Epaphras, our dear fellow servant, who is a faithful minister of Christ on your behalf.

In Colossians 4:7 we see the same affection being shown toward Tychicus:

> Tychicus, who is a beloved brother, a faithful minister, and a fellow servant in the Lord, will tell you all the news about me.

Notice the warmth expressed in these words — dear, faithful, beloved — yet the confidence he felt toward them as "fellow servants" was the highest compliment he could pay them. These three men shared a *sundoulous* ministry together in the Lord. Paul concluded his comments by telling the Colossians:

> Tychicus will tell you all the news about me (because he is my *sundoulous*).

First Corinthians 3:9 tells us: "For we are God's fellow workers;" and second Corinthians 6:1 describes us as "workers together with Him." We need never work alone — we have a *sundoulous* union with God. God's fellow workers!

With such a partnership, how can we not succeed? God will

equip us with everything needed for His service. We need to work as if everything depended upon God, so that God can depend on us. What a compliment God has given us in calling us "fellow workers with Him."

Oikonomos

Not only must we be servants, we are also called to be stewards. The Greek word for "steward" is *oiknonomos* which primarily denotes a manager of a household or estate.

> Let a man so consider us, as servants of Christ and stewards of the mysteries of God (1 Corinthians 4:1).

Have you ever thought that we are stewards in God's service? We are stewards or caretakers of God's business. The Lord has put into our hands a great work to accomplish.

I believe we as women have a special kind of stewardship. Our sphere of influence is far reaching, yet we come closest to fulfilling our stewardship by beginning in the place where we are. To "bloom where we are planted" is a God given privilege and honor. To find genuine fulfillment these days is not easy. I rarely find a truly contented woman (or man either, for that matter).

Perhaps it is because we've lost sight of our calling — to serve others. Christ came to serve and be an example for us. If we would be like Him, we must first learn to be content with what we have — then take care of *His* resources. This is our stewardship; this is our "holy ground."

We should always be grateful for the privilege that has been put into our keeping — that of being good stewards of the many facets of God's grace.

> As each one has received a gift, minister it to one another as good stewards of the manifold grace of God (1 Peter 4:10).

CHURCH OF CHRIST, EAST FRAYSER
2285 FRAYSER BLVD.
MEMPHIS, TN 38127
(901) 357-7444

Stewardship

Steward I . . . and not possessor . . . of the wealth
  entrusted me.
What, were God Himself the holder, would His
  disposition be?
Then I ask myself each morning, every noon
  and every night,
As I view His gentle goodness with an ever
  new delight.
Steward only . . . never owner . . . of the time that
  He has lent,
How, were He my life's custodian,
  would my years on earth be spent?

Then I ask myself each hour, as I plod my
  pilgrim way
Steeped in gratefulest amazement at His mercy
  day by day.
Steward only . . . not possessor . . . of the part
  of Him that's I.
Clearer grows this truth, and dearer, as the years
  go slipping by.
May I softly go, and humbly, head and heart
  in reverence bent,
That I may not fear to show Him how my
  stewardship was spent.

— Author Unknown

CHAPTER ONE

SOMETHING TO THINK ABOUT TODAY

1. Paul called himself a _____ ____ _____.
2. The term "servant" is not so much a title as a _____.
3. "Doulous" is the Greek word for _____.
4. What does "doulous" mean?
5. Discuss why being a servant qualifies one as being great.
6. Satan held us in bondage to sin, until _____ set us free.
7. Discuss why "standing fast in the liberty by which Christ set us free" is important.
8. What is the meaning of the Greek term "diakanos?"
9. A minister, deacon or elder is living a lie who only desires _____ never _____.
10. The Greek word "sundoulos" means _____ _____.
11. How do the verses in 1 Corinthians 3:9 and 2 Corinthians 6:1 describe our service?
12. The Greek word for "steward" is "oiknonomos" which denotes a manager of ____ _____ _____ _____.

CHAPTER TWO

SERVING GOD IN THE SPIRIT

In Romans 1:8 and 9, Paul wrote to the Christians in Rome:

> First, I thank my God through Jesus Christ for you all, that your faith is spoken of throughout the whole world. For God is my witness, whom I serve with my spirit in the gospel of His son, that without ceasing I make mention of you always in my prayers, . . .

Paul said he served God with his *spirit*. What did he mean? Can we also serve God in this way?

The Spirit of God

We know that God is Spirit for in Genesis 1:27 we read this remarkable truth:

> So God created man in His own image; in the image of God He created him; male and female He created them.

God created men and women equal in the sense they are both created in His image. The spirit is the part of us made in the image of God — the part of us which will never die. The spirit will live eternally.

The spirit within a Christian woman's heart longs for and reaches out for God. This longing was placed within every human heart and has a great capacity to grow in understanding of God.

> . . . that He would grant you, according to the riches of His glory, to be strengthened with might

through His spirit in the inner man . . . (Ephesians 3:16).

The Spirit's Home

God's Spirit must have a dwelling place, so the Spirit makes His home in our hearts. Our bodies furnish the dwelling place which houses the Spirit. Consequently we must take the very best care of our bodies. Paul wisely admonishes us in 1 Corinthians 6:19 and 20:

> Or do you not know that your body is the temple of the Holy spirit who is in you, whom you have from God, and you are not your own? For you were bought at a price; therefore glorify God in your body and in your spirit, which are God's.

Our bodies belong to God, housing this most precious commodity — God's Spirit. At the time of this writing, the Corinthians had not learned the tremendous fact that their bodies were the temples of the Holy Spirit.

We have been given the marvelous privilege of glorifying God in our bodies and in our spirits, "which are God's." We are not our own.

We, as Christian women, seek to please our heavenly Father through physical and spiritual service. We want to glorify Him in all we think and do.

Romans 12:1 and 2, are the criteria for all spiritual service:

> I beseech you therefore, brethren, by the mercies of God, that you present your bodies a living sacrifice, holy, acceptable to God, which is your reasonable service. And do not be conformed to this world, but be transformed by the renewing of your mind, that you may prove what is that good and acceptable and perfect will of God.

Our bodies are to be offered as living sacrifices. A sacrifice which stays alive requires consistent nourishment and feeding. We are to be "formed in Christ" until our minds are wholly renewed and transformed. This is God's plan and will. Others can test God's will by the amount of reasonable service they see demonstrated daily in our lives.

The Divine Spark

The spirit then is the inner person designed to be the dwelling place of God. I like to call it the *divine spark within*. Peter, the apostle of Christ, who was radically transformed, shares the wonderful good news that "we may be partakers of the divine nature" (2 Peter 1:4). This is as great a gift as any of us can receive. It comes about only when we allow the Holy Spirit to dwell within.

The Holy Spirit is a gift received at the point of repentance and baptism. Peter told the Jews on the day of Pentecost:

> Repent, and let every one of you be baptized in the name of Jesus Christ for the remission of sins; and you shall receive the gift of the Holy Spirit (Acts 2:38).

Every human born into this world is a living soul (the Bible also refers to it as the hidden man of the heart). We can only come alive and fulfill our purpose when the soul has been sparked by the Holy Spirit.

It is like a fireplace. The wood is there — but it is not going to flare up and burn until it has been lit by a match. So it is with the human spirit as well.

> A man found frost upon his windows and tried to scrape it off. A neighbor saw him. "What are you doing?" he asked. "Getting rid of the frost" said the other, "for I can't see out." His friend saw it was foolish and slow work, so quietly said, "Light a fire inside, and the frost will disappear of itself." How wise this remark, and if our hearts and lives have got chilled by the cold atmosphere of doubt and reason, ask God to light the fire of his love within us, and soon there will be warmth and light and joy, in both heart and life.
>
> — Author Unknown

An Old Irish Blessing

May the blessing of light be on you,
Light without and within.
May the blessed sunshine shine on you
And warm your heart till it glows like a great peat fire,
So the stranger may come and warm himself at it,
And also a friend.

And may the light shine out of the two eyes of you
Like a candle set in two windows of a house,
Bidding the wanderer to come in out of the storm.

And may the blessing of the rain be on you —
The soft sweet rain.
May it fall upon your spirit
So that all the little flowers may spring up,
And shed their sweetness on the air.

And may the blessing of the earth be on you —
The great round earth.
May you ever have a friendly greeting for
Them you pass
As you are going along the roads.

May the earth be soft under you when
You rest upon it,
Tired at the end of the day,
And may it rest easy over you
When, at the last, you lay out under it.
May it rest so lightly over you
That your soul may be out from under
It quickly —
And up and off and on its way to God.

— Author Unknown

It is the inner spirit which helps us understand spiritual things. The Holy Spirit enlightens our understanding. Romans 8:9 clarifies this truth:

> But you are not in the flesh but in the Spirit, if indeed the Spirit of God dwells in you. Now if

anyone does not have the Spirit of Christ, he is not His.

Romans 8:16 goes on to say:

> The Spirit Himself bears witness with our Spirit that we are children of God.

It is the hidden self (the spirit) which prays and communes with God:

> Praying always with all prayer and supplication in the spirit (Ephesians 6:18).

Alfred Lloyd Tennyson expressed it so well:

> Speak to Him for He heareth
> And spirit to Spirit can speak;
> Closer is He than breathing —
> And nearer than hands and feet.

In the Spirit's power we serve God and mankind. We are created for one purpose — to serve and glorify God and to serve His created beings. That's why we are here — that's what life is all about!

> For we are His workmanship (work of art) created in Christ Jesus for good works, which God prepared beforehand that we should walk in them (Ephesians 2:10).

Let Me Give

I do not know how long I'll live
   But while I live, Lord, let me give
Some comfort to someone in need
   By smile or nod . . . kind word or deed.

And let me do what e'er I can
   To ease things for my fellow man
I want nought but to do my part
   To lift a tired or weary heart.

> To change folks frowns
> To smiles again ...
> Then I will not have lived in vain
> And I'll not care how long I'll live
> If I can give — and give — and give.
>
> —Author Unknown

Someone has said: "The measure of a man is not the amount of servants he has, but the kind of servant he is."

Job asks a curious question in Job 38:36:

> Who has put wisdom in the mind?
> Or who has given understanding to the heart?

David answers this question in Psalm 51:6:

> Behold, You desire truth in the inward parts,
> And in the hidden parts You will make me to know wisdom.

Thank God for His precious workings in the inner spirit of man.

The Spirit of Man

> "The spirit of man is the lamp of the Lord, searching all the inner depths of his heart" (Proverbs 20:27).

Jesus described John the Baptist in this manner:

> "He was a burning and shining lamp" (John 5:35).

Before any lamp or candle can shine, it must be ignited by fire. There must be a burning. The writer of Proverbs says that God depends upon His people's spirits to be this world's light.

Do you remember how Jeremiah described the Word of God?

> Then I said: "I will not make mention of Him,
> Nor speak anymore in His name."
> But His Word was in my heart like a burning fire
> Shut up in my bones;

> I was weary of holding it back,
> And I could not (Jeremiah 20:9).

The word of God is that which feeds the spirit of man and causes him to shine. We have been sparked by the Holy Spirit — set on fire by the Lord, thus we become this world's light. The physical, mental and emotional parts of our nature depend on the spirit part of us for light and direction. No person can truly be blessed and helped, unless we, as servants, have been lit by God. Then and only then can we be lamps for the Lord to shine out this world's darkness.

Fill Us

> This is the secret of the holy,
> Not our holiness but HIM:
> Jesus! empty us and fill us
> With Thy fullness to the brim.
>
> — Author Unknown

Helen Keller, who was blind and deaf said: "I long more than anything for my spirit to soar." She realized it was her spirit which superseded all her other senses. This was demonstrated in her beautiful life of service.

Two Ways to Serve God

> For this reason we also, since the day we heard it, do not cease to pray for you, and to ask that you may be filled with the knowledge of His will in all wisdom and spiritual understanding; that you may have a walk worthy of the Lord, fully pleasing Him, being fruitful in every good work and increasing in the knowledge of God (Colossians 1:9 and 10).

There are two ways we can perform our "good" works:

> In the flesh or . . .
> In the spirit.

We learn through the Scriptures that the spirit and the flesh are at enmity with one another — they have always been at war. We carry on a constant struggle everyday between the flesh and the spirit. The battle never ends. Galatians 5:16 and 17 makes this clear:

> I say then: Walk in the Spirit, and you shall not fulfill the lust of the flesh. For the flesh lusts against the Spirit, and the Spirit against the flesh; and these are contrary to one another, so that you do not do the things that you wish.

It is helpful to know that Paul endured the same struggles which confront us. He describes this warfare in Romans 7:18-25:

> For I know that in me (that is, in my flesh) nothing good dwells; for to will is present with me, but how to perform what is good I do not find. For the good that I will to do, I do not do; but the evil I will not to do, that I practice.
>
> Now if I do what I will not to do, it is no longer I who do it, but sin that dwells in me. I find then a law, that evil is present with me, the one who wills to do good.
>
> For I delight in the law of God according to the inward man. But I see another law in my members, warring against the law of my mind, and bringing me into captivity to the law of sin which is in my members.
>
> O wretched man that I am! Who will deliver me from this body of death?
>
> I thank God — through Jesus Christ! So then, with the mind I myself serve the law of God, but with the flesh the law of sin.

The practicability of performing good works is always with us, but summoning up the heart and spirit to actually put them in practice is another thing. The desire to do good separates us from our evil nature. We can either be controlled by the flesh or by the Spirit.

In the Flesh

When we serve God in the flesh, we do so, not as a privilege or pleasure, but as a duty. Serving God in the flesh we have a tendency to want our good deeds to be seen by men, not to glorify God, but rather, that we ourselves may be glorified. We want others to recognize what we have done — we want others to see that we have been very good.

> Take heed that you do not do your charitable deeds before men, to be seen by them. Otherwise you have no reward from your Father in heaven.
>
> Therefore, when you do a charitable deed, do not sound a trumpet before you as the hypocrites do in the synagogues and in the streets, that they may have glory from men.
>
> Assuredly, I say to you, they have their reward. But when you do a charitable deed, do not let your left hand know what your right hand is doing, that your charitable deed may be in secret, and your Father who sees in secret will Himself reward you openly (Matthew 6:1-4).

Our good deeds should be a secret — a secret between our Lord and us. Hadn't we rather have the reward of our Father who sees in secret than the open rewards of men?

Dr. Hudson in Lloyd C. Douglas' book *Magnificent Obsession*, discovered the principle of Matthew 5:3. It forever changed his life and became the guiding force which enabled him to serve. He wrote a journal in which he described this concept:

> Once you have touched it, you will never be able to let it go . . . if you are of the temperament that demands self-indulgence to keep you happy and confident enough to do your work — leave all this alone, and go your way! For if you make an excursion into this, you're bound! It will plaster a mortgage on everything you think you own, and commandeer your time when you might prefer to be using it for yourself . . . it is very expensive . . . it took the man who discovered it to a cross at the age of thirty-three!

In the Spirit

When we serve others with our spirit, what happens? We no longer care who gets the credit. We do not announce to others what we have done. We serve meekly and humbly, not for the praise, but because we want God's name to be glorified. We want to bestow on others a spiritual blessing.

Greenville Kleiser said:

> The practical value of any position of responsibility is in its opportunities of service rather than of gain. The truest service you can render is that which we do quietly and silently, and without expectation of gratitude or reward.

Someone has said, "There is nothing God will not do through one who does not care to whom the credit goes." God calls us to be light in this dark world (Matthew 5:16). He wants our good deeds to direct men's praise to Him, not ourselves.

Richard Foster, the author of *Celebration of Discipline* writes about the difference between self-righteous service and true service:

1. Self-righteous service comes through human effort. True service comes from a relationship with the divine Other deep inside.
2. Self-righteous service is impressed with the "big deal." True service finds it almost impossible to distinguish the small from the large service.
3. Self-righteous service requires external rewards. True service rests contented in hiddenness.
4. Self-righteous service is highly concerned about results. True service is free of the need to calculate results.
5. Self-righteous service picks and chooses whom to serve. True service is indiscriminate in its ministry.
6. Self-righteous service is affected by moods and whims. True service ministers simply and faithfully because there is a need.
7. Self-righteous service is temporary. True service is a life-style.
8. Self-righteous service is without sensitivity. True service can withhold the service as freely as perform it.
9. Self-righteous service fractures community. True service, on the other hand, builds community. It quietly and

unpretentiously goes about caring for the needs of others. It puts no one under obligation to return the service. It draws, binds, heals, builds. The result is the unity of the community.

Father, Where Shall I Work Today?

"Father, where shall I work today?"
And my love flowed warm and free,
And he pointed me out a tiny spot
And said "tend that for me."
I answered quickly, "Oh, no, not that
Why, no one would ever see
No matter how well my work was done
Not that little place for me."

The word he spoke, it was not stern;
He answered tenderly,
"Little one, search that heart of thine;
Art thou working for them or me?
Nazareth was a little place
And so was Galilee."

— Author Unknown

CHAPTER TWO

SOMETHING TO THINK ABOUT TODAY

1. In Romans 1:8 and 9, Paul said he served God with His _____.
2. The spirit is the part of us made in the _____ ___ _____. It is the part of us which will never _____.
3. Ephesians 3:16 tells us that we can be _____ ___ _____ through His spirit ___ _____ _____ _____.
4. Where does God's Spirit make His home?
5. Why is it necessary for us to take the very best care of our bodies?
6. 1 Corinthians 6:19 and 20 tell us:
   A. The body is _____ _____ ___ _____ _____ _____ _____ ___ ___ _____.
   B. The Spirit is ___ _____.
   C. You are not your _____.
   D. You were bought at a _____.
   E. Therefore glorify God in your _____ and in your _____, which are _____.
7. Discuss Romans 12:1 and 2 and tell why these verses are the criteria of all spiritual service.
8. What is referred to as "the divine spark within?"
9. Every human born in this world is a _____ _____.
10. How does the Christian servant "come alive?"
11. Why is the soul or spirit of a Christian servant likened to a fireplace?
12. Why were we created?
13. Ephesians 2:10 tells us that we are His _____ created in Christ Jesus for _____ _____.
14. What is it that feeds the spirit of man and causes him to shine?
15. Name the two ways we can serve God. Describe the difference.
16. When we serve God in the flesh, we have a tendency to _____ _____ _____ _____ ___ ___ _____.
17. Why should we keep our good deeds a secret?
18. When we serve others with our spirit, what happens?
19. God calls us to be the _____ in this _____. He wants our _____ _____ to direct men's praise to _____ not _____.

CHAPTER 3

A WILLING SPIRIT

The first quality a Christian must attain in order to develop the servant's spirit is:

A Willing Spirit

A willing spirit usually denotes a strong purpose or intent. After Paul told the Christians at Rome that he always made mention of them in his prayers, he added these words:

> I long to see you so that I may impart to you some spiritual gift to make you strong — that is, that you and I may be mutually encouraged by each other's faith (Romans 1:11,12) NIV.

What a marvelous concept! Paul didn't write: "I'm so anxious to come to you because I know how much you can do for me." He couldn't wait to do something for them. He desired to bless their lives with a spiritual blessing. He ached in his heart to share with them. Paul had a willing spirit which *longed* to serve others.

To long for something is to have a strong yearning, a great desire, an earnest wish — it is to want something with all your heart.

We cannot bestow spiritual gifts the way Paul did, but we can give the spiritual gift of encouragement.

Paul's motive in bestowing spiritual gifts on the Romans was two-fold:

1. He wanted to strengthen them.
2. He desired mutual encouragement.

"... mutually encouraged by each other's faith...." These words need not only to be underlined in our Bibles, they need to be underlined in our hearts. Our growing faith sustains us personally, but it does something more as well. Our faith encourages others! To be "mutually encouraged" is a beautiful blessing. When we encourage others, our faith in God grows stronger, thus both you and I are enabled to serve in more effective ways. We'll spend more time later on in this book discussing the ministry of encouragement.

A Willingness To Serve

A spirit of willingness does not come naturally. We are born with the inclination to serve self and self is a hard master to conquer.

Deep within the heart of every Christian there must be cultivated a willingness to serve. Any service performed without a willingness to do so, will be performed grudgingly and without heart. The truth of its sham and pretense will be discovered in due time.

It is touching to observe the transformation in the apostle Peter. A man once consumed by selfish, impulsive, impetuous desires, he grew into a caring, dedicated servant of God. His servant heart came from being with and following the greatest servant of all — His Lord and Master Jesus Christ.

Likewise, in his first book, Peter exhorted the elders in this manner:

> To the elders among you, I appeal as a fellow elder, a witness of Christ's sufferings and one who also will share in the glory to be revealed. Be shepherds of God's flock that is under your care, serving as overseers — not because you must, but because you are willing, as God wants you to be; not greedy for money, but eager to serve; not lording it over those entrusted to you, but being examples to the flock (1 Peter 5:1-3) NIV.

We, as members of His body should take this admonition to heart . . . seeking to serve others "not because we must, but because we are willing." A sense of obligation to "do our duty" will get us started off on the wrong foot.

At times it is necessary to *make* ourselves serve. Before long, we shall find that the service we dreaded is a blessing in disguise. 2 Corinthians 5:14 is a lovely verse to memorize and heed:

"For the love of Christ constrains us..."

The love of Christ is a powerful motivator. We remember the service He rendered in dying for our sins. Any service, no matter how big or small, cannot begin to measure up to His. The love of Christ within the heart should be the motivating force behind every act of service. Someone has said: "The willingness of Jesus to give Himself for us should compel us to give ourselves in service to Him."

> A missionary is said to have been asked if he liked his work in Africa. His reply: "Do I like this work? No. My wife and I do not like the dirt. We have reasonably refined sensibilities. We do not like crawling into vile huts through goat-stands. We do not like association with ignorant, filthy, brutish people. But is a man to do nothing for Christ except what he likes? God pity him if not. Liking or disliking has nothing to do with it. We have orders to go, and we go. Love constrains us."
>
> — Author Unknown

During the last hours of Jesus' trial and suffering, His apostles had difficulty in coping with the anguish and pain their Master was experiencing. Jesus went apart to pray, then turned to find Peter, James and John sleeping. He said to Peter:

> Watch and pray, lest you enter into temptation.
> The spirit indeed is willing, but the flesh is weak
> (Matthew 26:41).

Let's face it! The flesh is weak. The flesh is reluctant to serve. The flesh does not want to be inconvenienced.

"If it's convenient," we say, "and we have the time, and don't have anything else planned, we'll take a casserole to Thelma who is sick in bed." Many acts of service are left undone because we hate to be inconvenienced.

Think how many acts of service we have rationalized away because we were too tired, not in the mood, had too much to do, or we figured something else was more important. We put off making a telephone call or visit, writing a note, or listening to somebody's troubles, because we do not have a willing, yielded spirit. Discouragement weakens us — the flesh gets in the way, so we postpone doing a good deed.

A Yielded Spirit

A willing spirit is a yielded spirit . . . an attitude we certainly need to cultivate. The whole point of yielding our bodies as living sacrifices is so God can work through us fully.

Mary, the mother of Jesus, had the most yielded and willing spirit of any woman we read about in the Bible. I am sure this is why God chose her to be the mother of our Lord.

When she learned the astonishing news that she had been chosen to bear the son of God, she reacted with a sublime submission that should characterize our acceptance and obedience to God's plan.

> Then Mary said: "Behold the handmaid of the Lord; be it unto me according to thy word (Luke 1:38) KJV.

The NIV renders it:

> I am the Lord's servant, may it be to me as you have said.

This Scripture is followed by these simple words:

> "Now Mary arose . . . and went . . ." (verse 39).

A handmaid or maidservant in Bible times was a female slave. On the scale or servanthood, she held the lowest position. She had no rights or privileges of her own — she was to submit totally to her superior. The term implies humility and compliance. Mary accepted God's will for her life even though she was far from understanding it. With her heart yielded and obedient, she said, "Be it unto me according to Your Word."

Yes, God had a great plan for young Mary, and He has a plan for our lives too. May we truly desire to live in the will of God in ways that He knows best.

Elizabeth, the mother of John, recognized Mary's yielded attitude. Upon Mary's visit, she whispered reverently:

> Blessed is she who believed, for there will be a fulfillment of those things which were told her from the Lord (Luke 1:45).

Once we know God's will for our lives, we have a heavenly calling to live submissively to our Master's will.

> And that servant who knew his master's will, and did not prepare himself or do according to his will, shall be beaten with many stripes. But he who did not know, yet committed things worthy of stripes, shall be beaten with few. For everyone to whom much is given, from him much will be required; and to whom much has been committed, of him they will ask the more (Luke 12:47 and 48).

The Source of a Willing Spirit

A willing, yielded spirit comes from within the heart. Read this wonderful Scripture found in Psalm 45:13, KJV.

> The king's daughter is all glorious within . . .

All glorious within! What does that mean? It means "to be filled with glory!" Whose glory? HIS. We actually carry His glory around in us! The light that shines upon our faces comes from the radiance within. Where does it come from? This radiant glory comes from looking at Christ (through His Word).

> But we all, with unveiled face, beholding as in a mirror the glory of the Lord, are being transformed into the same image from glory to glory, just as by the Spirit of the Lord (2 Corinthians 3:18).

The more we look at Jesus, the more we'll become like Him, and the brighter our faces will shine. I love the verse found in Psalm 34:5:

> They looked to Him and were radiant, And their faces were not ashamed.

I never will forget the day I discovered these splendid descriptions of those who look to the Lord. Do you want to be radiant, ladies? Look to Jesus — a special beauty secret.

> When a woman shines from within, she looks much younger than she really is; and her radiance doesn't come from the cosmetics on her face — it comes from the glow within.
>
> — Author Unknown

We must then conclude that our radiance and glow comes from the Lord living within. King's daughters? Indeed! When we are servants of the living Lord, we are daughters of the King! We are equipped for daily service by receiving His glory.

His glory has arisen upon us. We should arise and shine. Every day of our lives we should be excited about arising and shining. This should be a verse to which we can respond morning by morning.

> Arise, shine;
> For your light has come!
> And the glory of the Lord
> is risen upon you (Isaiah 60:1).

Our glory is like the moon which reflects the radiance of the sun. We are all reflectors of someone. May our reflection always mirror His image.

One evening, unable to sleep, I pondered this question: How can one reconcile being a "handmaid of the Lord" and a "daughter of the King?" Then the answer came to me.

A handmaid is a position we choose to take for Him. A daughter of the King is a position He chooses for us! We honor Him by saying, "I will be your handmaid." He honors us by saying "You are my daughters."

Perhaps that is why Peter calls us a "royal priesthood" in 1 Peter 2:9:

> But you are a chosen generation, a royal priesthood, a holy nation, His own special people, that you may proclaim the praises of Him who called you out of darkness into His marvelous light.

Scriptures Concerning the Willing Spirit

A study of the scriptures enlightens our understanding about the necessity of having a willing spirit or heart:

1. "Then the Lord spoke to Moses, saying: Speak to the children of Israel, that they bring Me an offering. From everyone who gives it willingly with his heart you shall take My offering" (Exodus 25:1 and 2).

    (From this passage of scripture we find that God has always desired a willing spirit *within the hearts* of His people.)

2. "Take from among you an offering to the Lord. Whoever is of a willing heart, let him bring it as an offering to the Lord:" (Exodus 35:5).

    (These verses were written at the time the tabernacle was being constructed. God asked a willing offering from the people. A free-will offering of our services would greatly enhance our ministries. Wouldn't it be wonderful if everything we did was offered from the heart?

3. "When leaders lead in Israel, When the people willingly offer themselves, Bless the Lord!" (Judges 5:2).

    (This was a portion of a song that Deborah and Barek sang to the Lord. The 9th verse of this chapter sums up God's response to the yielded attitude of Israel's leaders: "My heart is with the rulers of Israel who offered themselves willingly with the people.")

4. "As for you, my son Solomon, know the God of your Father, and serve Him with a loyal heart and with a willing mind; for the Lord searches all hearts and understands all the intent of the thoughts (1 Chronicles 28:9).

    (Our good intentions are known by God. Would that all good intentions were carried out! When Solomon inherited the throne of Israel, David admonished his son to serve the Lord with a loyal heart and willing mind. Our faithfulness to God demands that our minds be yielded to His will.)

5. "Your people shall be volunteers in the day of Your power; In the beauties of holiness from the womb of the morning . . ." (Psalm 110:3).

    (It is interesting to read Webster's definition of a volunteer: "A person who enters or offers to enter into any service of his own free will." God needs volunteers in His mighty army, doesn't He? A voluntary act denotes submissiveness. It means that we freely choose to serve. No one has coerced us — we serve because we want to.)

6. "She seeks wool and flax, and willingly works with her hands" (Proverbs 31:13).
   (We recognize this description of the worthy woman. She applies herself willingly, with a yielded heart to her tasks. She is not slothful or indifferent toward her work. She counts it a privilege and blessing to be able to work with her hands. Perhaps, if the use of our hands were taken away for a few days, we would appreciate the blessing of having hands with which to do our work. Such an experience would cause us to have more submissive minds.
7. "If you are willing and obedient, You shall eat of the good of the land" (Isaiah 1:19). (Notice how often willingness is coupled with obedience? Certainly obedience to God depends upon a person's willingness to be obedient. Do you recall how disappointed Samuel was when Saul disobeyed? He spared Agag and the best of the sheep, the oxen, the fatlings, the lambs and all that was good. He was unwilling to destroy them even though God had commanded him to do so.)

    Saul offered this excuse:

    > . . . the people spared the best of the sheep and the oxen, to sacrifice to the Lord your God; and the rest we have utterly destroyed" (1 Samuel 15:15).

    Then Samuel said:

    > Has the Lord as great delight in burnt offerings and sacrifices,
    > As in obeying the voice of the Lord?
    > Behold, to obey is better than sacrifice (1 Samuel 15:22).
    > (Saul was unwilling to be obedient to God. He possessed a stubborn spirit which wanted to have his own way. How often have we ourselves sung "Have Thine Own Way" and then spent the rest of the day seeking "our way?")

8. "Moreover, brethren, we make known to you the grace of God bestowed on the churches of Macedonia: that in a great trial of affliction the abundance of their joy and their

deep poverty abounded in the riches of their liberality. For I bear witness that according to their ability, yes, and beyond their ability, they were freely willing . . . And this they did, not as we had hoped, but first gave themselves to the Lord, and then to us by the will of God" (2 Corinthians 8:1-3 and 5).

(The Macedonians gave from liberal hearts which had already decided to place God first. Until we, first of all give ourselves, the gift lacks that which is needed most — the willing spirit. We can give everything we own, but until we give ourselves we have sacrificed little.)

9. "For if there is first a willing mind, it is accepted according to what one has, and not according to what he does not have" (2 Corinthians 8:12).

(I believe with all my heart there must be a willing mind before genuine service comes about. The ability to serve is fine, but the willingness to serve is seen and appreciated by others and most of all by God.)

Ready Unto Every Good Work

The following thoughts written by Harvey Porter are convicting:

> The children of God should not have to be begged to do His work. No child of God should be begged to give to the work of Jesus, to come and worship on the Lord's Day, to visit and help his fellow Christians whom he loves. He is a "self-starter" spiritually. His love for Jesus and His church motivates him to do what needs to be done when he sees it. He would not entertain the thought that if he waits maybe someone else in the church will do it. He is "ready unto every good work" (2 Timothy 2:21).
>
> Let's not have to be pushed, threatened, scared, or begged to *move* for Jesus.

I recommend the following admonitions given to Timothy by Paul:

> Command those who are rich in this present age not to be haughty, nor to trust in uncertain riches

but in the living God, who gives us richly all things to enjoy. Let them do good, that they be rich in good works, ready to give, willing to share, storing up for themselves a good foundation for the time to come, that they may lay hold on eternal life (1 Timothy 6:17-19).

We who have been given so much from God should have a willing spirit, *ready* to give; eager to share. By so doing, we are laying up for ourselves the blessings of eternal life.

Luke 12:35 is a wonderful verse. It would be well to underline it in our Bibles. "Be dressed ready for service and keep your lamps burning." NIV

Isn't that a fantastic verse? The New King James Version renders it this way: "Let your waist be girded and your lamp burning."

"To be girded" in Bible times meant that one was not only ready and prepared; but was equipped and expectant. I believe God will send us opportunities for service in proportion to our willingness.

A speaker at the Tulsa Soul Winning Workshop said that every morning she dressed herself from tip to toe as if she might be called upon at any time to go out and serve someone. She arrayed herself in a suitable outfit, hose and shoes.

In addition, she fixed her hair and put on her make-up. If someone called with a need, she was ready to go!

The Best That I Can

"I cannot do much," said a little star,
"To make the dark world bright;
My silver beams cannot struggle far
Through the folding gloom of night;
But I am a part of God's great plan,
And I'll cheerfully do the best that I can."

"What is the use," said a fleecy cloud,
"Of these dew-drops that I hold?
They will hardly bend the lily proud
Though caught in her cup of gold;
Yet I am a part of God's great plan,
My treasures I'll give as well as I can."

A child went merrily forth to play,
But a thought, like a silver thread,
Kept winding in and out all day
Through the happy, busy head,
Mother said, "Darling, do all you can,
For you are a part of God's great plan!"

So she helped a younger child along,
When the road was rough to the feet;
And she sang from her heart a little song,
A song that was passing sweet;
And her father, a weary, toil-worn man,
Said, "I, too, will do the best that I can."

— Author Unknown

"I am but one, but I am one, I cannot do everything, but I can do something. What I can do, by the grace of God, I will do."

— Author Unknown

CHAPTER THREE

SOMETHING TO THINK ABOUT TODAY

1. The first quality a Christian must attain in order to develop the servant's spirit is ____ _____ _____.
2. Describe the nature of a willing spirit.
3. What were Paul's motives in bestowing spiritual gifts on the Romans? Name two.
4. We are born with an inclination to serve _____.
5. Where did Peter obtain his servant heart?
6. At times it is necessary to _____ ourselves serve.
7. What is the motivating force behind every act of service?
8. Many acts of service are left undone because we hate to be _____.
9. What is the whole point of yielding our bodies as living sacrifices?
10. In a few words describe how Mary's statement in Luke 1:38 applies to us as Christian servants today.
11. Where does a willing, yielded heart come from?
12. A handmaid is a position ___ _____ _____ _____. A daughter of the King is a position ___ _____ _____ _____.
13. What is Webster's definition of a volunteer?
    A voluntary act denotes _____.
    It means that we are _____ ___ _____.
14. In God's Word willingness is coupled with _____.
15. The Macedonians gave from _____ _____ which had already decided to _____ _____ _____.
16. Why must genuine service be preceded by a willing mind?
17. Freely discuss Luke 12:35. Why is it significant?

CHAPTER FOUR

AN UNSELFISH SPIRIT

We must cultivate an unselfish spirit.
The Prayer that David prayed in Psalm 51:10 should be our prayer too:

> Create in me a clean heart, O God; and renew a right spirit within me. (KJV)

A *right* spirit is an unselfish spirit. All problems in relationships are due to selfishness. Wanting to please self rather than wanting to serve others is due to one basic attitude: selfishness.

How many times have I prayed David's prayer when I have felt my attitude to be wrong. I know many times my spirit is not right. I remember when our children were growing up in our home. There were numerous times when I could not put my finger on what was causing a developing problem. Somehow I knew that the problem had to do with either the children's attitude or my own. Don't you just love people with beautiful attitudes? I admire and appreciate a person's unselfish attitude more than his or her character. In fact, a person's character has a lot to do with her attitude.

Attitudes

All attitudes are determined a great deal by the spirit within each of us. It is true for the most part that we choose our own attitudes. It may be an unconscious act but netherless it is true. If we have a bad attitude and a selfish spirit, nine times out of ten, we have chosen to be that way.

Someone has said, "Most of us can do more than we think we can, if only we would give ourselves the chance. The attitude within us is more important than the circumstances without."

One important point to remember when we are striving to form good attitudes is to *never allow someone else to determine our own attitude.*

It is so easy for someone to come along and "hit" us the wrong way. Perhaps they say a harsh word or have a negative spirit. We hear someone gossiping about another, running someone down; what should be our attitude? It is so tempting for us to join in, participating, doing our part to run down another person too.

Is this the attitude God wants us to take? No. He wants our spirits to soar above this. He wants our attitudes to be bigger, finer, deeper, more in control. And we can be, if we pray that God will give us a "clean heart and a right spirit."

When we are feeling depressed or low in spirit, we may not *feel* like serving the Lord, but He can give us an attitude alteration.

When Paul told the Philippians, "Let this mind be in you which was also in Christ Jesus," he was really saying, "Your attitude should be the same as that of Christ Jesus" (Philippians 2:5). In fact, that is the way the New International Version translates this verse. It is a mind set, isn't it?

Wouldn't we all have better relationships if our speech and actions were determined by how Christ would speak and act? If we would talk like Him, act like Him, make choices like Him, and serve like Him, wouldn't we live differently? Wouldn't God be glorified? We need to pray for this kind of attitude. What was Christ's attitude? How would you describe it? He had the spirit of service to such a degree that He was willing to give up His equality with God! (verse 6). He was willing to empty Himself, taking upon Himself the very nature of a servant (verse 7).

What does "taking the nature (or form)" of a servant mean? It means He threw out all rights He possessed as very God! He gave us His right and power to be served and exalted. Instead, He deliberately chose the life of a *doulous* — a bond slave. "I am among you as one who serves," He said.

In so doing, He humbled Himself and became obedient to death, even the death of the cross (verse 8). The unselfish spirit that Christ manifested in the flesh is our highest example.

We ought to saturate our minds and hearts with the words in Philippians 2:1-11, until we know them by heart. Yet, after all is said and done, practicing these concepts is more important. Practicing the attitude of Christ will cause us to change our minds!

Our Ministry — Christ's Ministry

Matthew 20:28 says:

> ... just as the Son of Man did not come to be served, but to serve, and to give His life a ransom for many.

Because of human frailties we would much prefer to be ministered unto rather than to minister. Yet when we look at our Savior, we realize the extreme difference between us. Christ's whole purpose in coming to live among sinful man was that He might serve (minister). This unselfish devotion of service led Him to give His life a ransom for many. Jesus was our supreme example and we should strive to imitate him in all acts of service.

> A disciple is not above his teacher, nor a servant above his master. It is enough for a disciple that he be like his teacher, and a servant like his master (Matthew 10:24,25).

Max Lucado defined Christian service in his book *God Came Near:*

> Christianity, in its purest form, is nothing more
> than seeing Jesus.
>
> Christian service, in its purest form, is nothing more
> than imitating him who we see.
>
> To see His Majesty and to imitate him,
> that is the sum of Christianity.

Many of us are just plain selfish! We are too self-willed to go to the trouble, stress and effort of helping others, must less to give our lives in devoted service. We haven't begun to understand the meaning of service until we are willing to die to self and find life in service. If every one in our congregations served like us, what kind of congregation would it be?

How Would It Be?

If every member in the church
Were just like me . . .
What kind of church would
His church be?

Would the yard be mowed,
Or the building cleaned,
Would the classes be taught,
Or the new-comers seen?

Would the pews be filled
When the saints did meet?
And would everyone sit
On the very last seat?

Would I refuse to give
Of all that I have been given,
Because with a brother
Or sister I have striven?

Would I bury my talents
Deep in the sand,
And always refuse
To give a helping hand?

Would I use my tongue
To pray and to sing?
Or to plant evil thoughts
And unhappiness bring?

Would I smile and be happy
And praise my God each day?
Or frown and complain,
Be a stumbling block along the way?

Would I fix the communion,
And drive the bus?
Would I tend to the sick?
Or just grumble and fuss.

Would I hold up the hands
Of the young and the old?
Encourage their deeds,
Or grow bitter and cold?

I am not a puppet
On a string
God has told me
I can do anything.

Will that "anything" be
What He wants me to do?
It is my choice
What about you?

If every member in the church
Were just like you and me . . .
What kind of church
Would His church be?

— Joyce Girouard

Self-Denial

Jesus told His disciples in Mark 8:34 and 35:

> Whoever desires to come after Me, let him deny himself, and take up his cross, and follow Me. For whoever desires to save his life will lose it, but whoever loses his life for My sake and the gospel's will save it.

Denying self is not only one of the conditions of discipleship, it is also one of the conditions of servanthood . . . in fact, probably the number one condition. Paul said, "I die daily" (1 Corinthians 15:31). We also must die daily as we fight the old, selfish nature which laments "Take care of self first." How many times have we had to battle sinful, selfish and fleshly attitudes?

Our service needs to be heart-felt and unselfish. We put off doing what our hearts tell us to do. When we rise above the selfishness which lurks beneath the surface, how blessed we will be, and others will benefit.

I keep the following words attached to my refrigerator, so that I may see them often as a reminder to forget self:

Dying to Self

When you are forgotten, or neglected, or purposely set at naught, and you don't sting and hurt with the insult or the oversight, but your heart is happy, being counted worthy to suffer for Christ, that is DYING TO SELF.

When your good is evil spoken of, when your wishes are crossed, your advice disregarded, your opinions ridiculed, and you refuse to let anger rise in your heart, or even defend yourself, but take it all in patient, loving silence, that is DYING TO SELF.

When you lovingly and patiently bear any disorder, any irregularity, any impunctuality, or any annoyance; when you can stand face to face with waste, folly, extravagance, spiritual insensibility ... and endure it as Jesus endured it, that is DYING TO SELF.

When you are content with any food, any offering, any raiment, any climate, any society, any solitude, any interruption by the will of God, that is DYING TO SELF.

When you no longer care to hear yourself in conversation, or to record your own good works, or itch after commendation, when you can truly love to be unknown, that is DYING TO SELF.

When you can see your brother prosper and have his needs met, and can honestly rejoice with him in spirit and feel no envy nor question God, while your own needs are far greater and in desperate circumstance, that is DYING TO SELF.

When you can receive correction and reproof from one of less stature than yourself, and can humbly submit inwardly as well as outwardly, finding no rebellion or resentment rising up within your heart, that is DYING TO SELF.

— Author Unknown

Until we allow Him to have complete control of our lives, we will never understand what it means to die to self.

The More We Give, the Happier We Will Be.

Let us joyfully and unselfishly serve others. The more we give ourselves in service, the happier our lives will become. We will enjoy our Christian lives so much more. Our own load of griefs and burdens will seem lighter as we help to relieve the sufferings of others. Caring for others helps us forget our own problems.

I believe that caring leads to sharing.

> Once there was a king who was very worried and fearful that as he was getting older a revolution would throw him from his throne. So every morning he would stand before a huge mirror and look at himself to see if he looked old and weak. His counselor, a wise and godly man, told him he should be more concerned about his people instead of himself. But he didn't get the message.
>
> Conditions became desperate in his kingdom. One night the king's advisor slipped into his room and took the mirror out. He had a hole cut in the wall and replaced it with clear glass and turned the mirror into a window. The next morning the king got up to look at himself and instead he saw an old woman bent under a load of sticks. He saw little children scrounging for crusts of bread in the gutter. And he saw an old man limping with a wound. His heart went out to these people.
>
> "What is wrong with my people?" he cried. He called to his highest echelons and said, "Take care of the old woman. Give bread to the children. Help that old man."
>
> Caring led to sharing when the mirror was turned into a window. If you are not joyful enough your mirror probbly needs a window.
>
> — Author Unknown

Yes, the most joyful people in the world are those who give, share and serve. Remember, faith without works is dead.

> If a brother or sister is naked and destitute of daily food, and one of you says to them, "Depart in peace, be warmed and filled," but you do not give them the things which are needed for the body, what does it profit? Thus also faith by itself, if it does not have works, is dead (James 2:15-17).

How to Be Miserable

Would you like to grow old gracefully, with dignity and beauty? Give yourself away in service to others! The secret is in forgetting self. On the other hand, if one sits around and does nothing, feeling sorry for oneself, he or she will grow grouchy, complaining and bitter. The most miserable elderly people are those who are having a life-time pity party. They care only for themselves and what others can do for them. Life has been severe and difficult along the way and they will make every effort to see that everyone knows this.

This kind of person can never be pleased no matter how much is done for them. They are like spoiled children, never satisfied, never grateful. They remind me of our four-year-old grandchild, Angel. She asked for a drink of water, which I gave her. However, she didn't like the cup I served it in; she wanted the pink one. When I gave her the water in the pink cup, she then wanted ice in it. I complied; then she decided she didn't want water, but wanted orange juice instead.

Elderly people, like this, sit miserably wrapped up in themselves — the most unhappy and unproductive people on the face of the earth.

> Like clouds and wind without rain is a man who boasts of gifts he does not give (Proverbs 25:14) (NIV).

Esteem Others Better Than Self

Paul admonished the Philippians in this manner:

> Let nothing be done through selfish ambition or conceit, but in lowliness of mind let each esteem others better than himself (Philippians 2:3).

The same word which Paul used for selfish ambition (eritheia) was used by Paul in Galatians 5:20, when he mentions the works of the flesh. Selfish ambition (or thinking more highly of oneself than he ought) is listed along side of adultery, fornication, envy, murder and the like. Furthermore, he says that "those who practice such things will not inherit the kingdom of God" (Galatians 5:21).

I love Paul's positive statement found in Philippians 5:4:

> Let each of you look out not only for his own interests, but also for the interests of others.

Paul is telling us here that it is all right to take care of our own interests, but at the same time we are to look out for the interests of others, too. A person who only looks out for number one is a self-centered person. "Take care of yourself!" we are told in today's society. Not so, in God's kingdom. It is not easy to esteem others better than ourselves, or to look out for their interests. Only the grace of God can enable us to have this attitude. "Have this attitude that was in Christ Jesus!" It is only possible when we appropriate *His* unselfish attitudes.

Any Christian woman who puts herself above others is not going to have the mind of Christ. The basic cause of self-interest is selfishness and pride. Paul said: "For I say through the grace given to me, to everyone who is among you, not to think of himself more highly than he ought to think, but to think soberly, as God has dealt to each one a measure of faith" (Romans 12:3).

Again in Romans 12:16 he says: "Be of the same mind toward one another. Do not set your mind on high things, but associate with the humble. Do not be wise in your own opinion."

Dr. Clyde Narrimore states that "Everyone wears a sign around his neck which says, 'Make me feel significant.' " Dale Carnegie made a similar remark when he wrote, "The deepest urge in human nature is the desire to be important."

Both of these statements cause us to realize how imperative it is to make others feel significant and important. All of us enjoy being recognized and praised, yet we need to get ourselves out of the way so that God may rightly receive the glory.

I'm Out Of Breath, Lord!

I'm out of breath, Lord . . .
From going the extra mile
  so often
  for so many.
My capacity to give feels
  drained
  washed out
  expended
  dried up.
I'm tired and I feel cheated.
I guess I want a chance to bask in
  praise
  recognition
  appreciation
  even acclaim.
Forgive this selfish introspection
Lord, and needless self-pity,
Misdirected, unjustified grudges,
And my complaining spirit.
Remind me that I, too
  make mistakes
  let people down
  act on selfish whims
Give me strength to keep on
  giving
  and loving
  and caring
  and serving
When no reward is in sight,
And when no one is there to say
Thanks. Let my joy be in doing the
  unrecognized job.
In Jesus Name, Amen.

— Author Unknown

How much happier our lives can be if only we will stop trying to get attention. Instead, let us start noticing and paying attention to others. William Gladson said that selfishness is the greatest curse of the human race.

"To love at all is to be vulnerable," C.S. Lewis stated. "If you must keep your heart intact, give it to no one," he continued.

"Lock it safely, carefully in the coffin of your selfishness, and it will be unbreakable."

A million needs await us "somewhere out there" in this hurting world. The hardest part is choosing among so *many* services!

Someone, Just Anyone.

She sat alone in an old people's home,
Lonely and old and gray;
She wished that someone, just anyone,
Would call on her that day. Did you?

He was far from home on foreign soil,
Feeling homesick, lonely and blue;
He wished that someone, just anyone,
Would write a letter, too. Did you?

Her loved one had died a few weeks ago,
So sad and broken hearted she sat;
She wished that someone, just anyone,
Would come to her house to chat. Did you?

She spent long hours, that teacher,
Giving the best she knew;
She wished that someone, just anyone,
Would speak just a brief, "thank you!" Did you?

He lay for days on his hospital bed,
The hours were long and hard;
He wished that someone, just anyone,
Would send him a cheery card. Did you?

She felt a stranger, that little bride
When with her husband to services she came;
She wished that someone, just anyone,
Would stop and call her by name. Did you?

He hoped he had recited his verse real well,
That little fellow you know;
He wished that someone, just anyone,
Would smile and tell him so. Did you?

That matter of Christian service,
We are living it day by day;
When we help someone, just anyone,
As we walk along life's way.

— Author Unknown

Paul stated in 2 Corinthians 4:5:

"We preach not ourselves, but Christ Jesus the Lord; and ourselves your servants for Jesus' sake." KJV

In and through all relationships, in all acts of service, in all conversations, we are to proclaim Jesus Christ. We are to call attention to Him, caring little about what people think of *us*. This is easier said than done; it is not an easy life to which we have been called. At a lectureship I attended at Abilene Christian University, I found these words written on a poster in the lobby of the University church:

Help Wanted-Servants!

Someone to do often undesirable work for the sake of others. Needs strong sense of self-worth in God's eyes and true compassion for others. Must be personally acquainted with the *Greatest Servant* of all, in order to continue His training. Work requires being on call 24 hours a day to meet the needs of family, friends, and even strangers. Must be willing to give up his rights. No experience necessary. Job begins today, where you are.

— Author Unknown

The joy of service will not be found in doing what we want to do, but in doing what He wants us to do. Jesus said in John 13:17, "If you know these things, happy are you if you do them."
As our minister, Charlie Kymes, says so often: "People don't care how much you know till they know how much you care."

Most assuredly, I say to you, unless a grain of wheat falls into the ground and dies, it remains alone; but if it dies, it produces much grain. He who loves his life will lose it, and he who hates his life in this world will keep it for eternal life. If anyone serves Me, let him follow Me; and where I am, there My servant will be also. If anyone serves Me, him My Father will honor (John 12:24-26).

Living for Others

Lord, let me live from day to day
In such a self-forgetting way,
That even when I kneel to pray
My prayer shall be for others.

Help me in all the work I do
To ever be sincere and true,
And know that all I do for you
Must needs be done for others.

And when my work on earth is done
And my new work in Heaven's begun,
May I forget the course I've won
While thinking still of others.

Others, Lord, yes others!
Let this my motto be,
Help me to live for others
That I may live like Thee!

— Author Unknown

Helen Keller said, "Life is exciting, but *most* exciting when lived for others."

CHAPTER FOUR

SOMETHING TO THINK ABOUT TODAY

1. All problems in relationships are due to _____.
2. All attitudes are determined a great deal by the _____ within us.
3. Do you agree or disagree that for the most part we choose our own attitudes?
4. What is the most important factor we need to remember in striving to form good attitudes?
5. How is it possible for God to alter our attitudes?
6. When Paul told the Philippians "Let this mind be in you which was in Christ Jesus," what was he really saying?
7. Name several ways our relationships could be improved?
8. How would you describe Christ's basic attitude?
9. Who was our supreme example in unselfish, devoted service?
10. We haven't begun to understand the meaning of service until we are willing to ____ ___ _____.
11. Paul said ____ _____ _____ in 1 Corinthians 15:31. What do you think he meant?
12. Name some ways we can grow old gracefully, with dignity and beauty.
13. If you cannot quote Philippians 2:3 from memory, commit it to your mind today. Share it with friends until it becomes a part of you.
14. Serving unselfishly will cause us to take four steps. Write them down here:
    A.
    B.
    C.
    D.
15. True or false? The joy of service is found in doing what we want to do.

CHAPTER FIVE

A SACRIFICIAL SPIRIT

Not only must we be willing to serve and be unselfish in our attitudes, we need to cultivate a sacrificial spirit. I doubt if little service is accomplished without sacrifice.

Servanthood Begins in the Heart

Any time we are involved with another person, we are saying in effect: "You are more important than anything else I could be doing at this time." Acceptable service begins with sacrifice (Romans 12:1).

The hardest part of service is having to sacrifice the time we'd rather be doing something else. This is also the sweetest part of service as well. We are nearly always glad when we have sacrificed even if it seems very insignificant.

I've had people to come into to my home, or call on the phone and say: "Judy, I know you are busy. I feel like I am taking your time." It is times like this when I need to reassure them: "You're being here or calling manifests a need. I want to help if I can."

We need to cultivate the gift of seeing a need where and when it exists. Nearly every person we meet has a need of some kind. If we have the sacrificial spirit we will try to meet these needs in tangible ways. It is so easy to be blinded or insensitive to other's needs. We can desensitize ourselves to the point where we could care less.

Fear of Involvement

Many times our problem is that we are afraid. Afraid of what? We are afraid to discover a person's needs, for fear of involvement.

In order for any of us to be servants, it may be necessary to become involved in another person's life on a personal basis. And not many of us are willing to do this.

Perhaps this is why so little is done in the realm of service. It takes too much of our energy, time and strength. It robs us of time we feel we need for ourselves. It is too much of a sacrifice. Because heart service requires involvement in other's problems and troubles, we are apt to say "We have enough problems of our own!"

If there is one person whom we would wish to emulate, it would be our Lord. He felt a deep involvement with every person He met. God has given us various abilities, talents and strengths, and we need to stop worrying about doing it on our own. Christ lives in us and helps us at our greatest need.

If we are frightened at the prospect of becoming involved in another's life, we need to remember that "Perfect love casts out all fear" (1 John 4:18).

Another wonderful verse is found in 2 Timothy 1:7:

> For God has not given us a spirit of fear, but of power and of love and a sound mind.

Biblical Truths

Jesus came to give His life as a ransom for many. Somewhere along the line, we may be required to give up that which matters the most for the sake of others. Let us memorize these verses:

> Let no one seek his own, but each one the other's well being (1 Corinthians 10:24).

> Let each of us please his neighbor for his good, leading to edification. For even Christ did not please Himself; (Romans 15:2,3).

> If anyone desires to be first, he shall be last of all and servant of all (Mark 9:35).

Sacrifice

When you have more than you can eat
to feed a stranger is no feat.
When you have more than you can spend
it isn't hard to give or lend.
Who gives but what he will never miss
will never know what giving is.
He will win few praises from his Lord
who does but what he can afford.
The widow's mite to heaven went . . .
because real sacrifice was meant.

— Edgar A Guest

Extravagant Devotion

Every time we see a need and pretend it doesn't exist, it becomes easier the next time to avoid involvement and resist that need. We ask ourselves, "What can I really do, anyway?"

It is so easy to excuse ourselves on one basis or another. When this happens, we become very adept at excuses. We need to develop a sensitivity which goes beyond our own needs — even time, energy and budget.

We need to develop an extravagant devotion to our Lord. There are simply not enough ways to show our love to the Father. We love Him best by showing love to His other children.

Can a young woman in love find enough ways to please her sweetheart? Love makes sacrifice seem unnecessary.

Love gives fervently, intensely and whole-heartedly, without any strings attached.

A Lesson in Giving

I subscribe to a cheerful, warm, upbeat little magazine which is appropriately called *Sunshine*. One day I read this little story and it lifted my heart:

A Lesson in Giving

My seven-year-old son had a rock that he cherished. He found it on a hike with my father about two years ago. It is dusted lightly with a glitter-like substance that gives off a golden cast, and with a little encouragement from Grandpa he truly believed it was gold. That rock had been in his protective custody ever since.

It was an uncomfortable Christmas, we all had the flu, consequently my shopping was rather last minute. It must have seemed to my children that I had not bought a gift for them to give their Grandma. One morning I woke up to find a tiny package wrapped under the tree. "This is a present for Grandma," my son said proudly. To my disbelief, he had wrapped his rock, his most precious possession, to give to her. He gave it purely and simply, without hesitation, motivated only by love.

I believe my son taught me something about giving that day. Could I give my most treasured possession to someone else so freely? I'm afraid my answer is rather embarrassing. If only we could give those things that are hardest to give — time, love, forgiveness; some significant part of ourselves that can truly be appreciated.

My mother keeps that rock in her china cabinet with her best crystal. On a sunny day, if the light shines through the window just right, it lets the rock give off a brilliant glow. It is there to remind us of that special Christmas when a little boy taught us that giving, in its most splendid moment, isn't something you buy from a store. Real giving costs a little bit more.

— Mary Morrone

The Alabaster Box of Service

There is a beautiful story told in the Bible which illustrates the sacrifice and devotion which should characterize our service for the Lord. It is found in Matthew 26:6-13:

> And when Jesus was in Bethany at the house of Simon the leper, a woman came to Him having an alabaster flask of very costly fragrant oil, and she poured it on His head as He sat at the table. But when His disciples saw it, they were indig-

nant, saying, "To what purpose is this waste? For this fragrant oil might have been sold for much and given to the poor." But when Jesus was aware of it, He said to them, "Why do you trouble the woman? For she has done a good work for Me. For you have the poor with you always, but Me you do not always have. For in pouring this fragrant oil on My body, she did it for My burial. Assuredly, I say to you, wherever this gospel is preached in the whole world, what this woman has done will also be told as a memorial to her."

How indignant the disciples were. "This is such a waste!" they stated. "That oil could have been sold for a fortune and given to the poor." Jesus commended her by saying, "Why do you make a fuss over here? She has performed a good work upon me."

There will always be people who criticize our efforts. We must not let that stand in the way of service for our Lord. Any service that we do for other people should cost us something in personal sacrifice.

This woman's service was not only an act of good works, but an act of devotion. It was set to the tune of love. The "song" she sang for the Lord that day will be told throughout the ages as an example of service performed with winsomeness. Though notes of that song were mingled with tears, the melody was harmonious and beautiful. Even now in the 20th century, we as Christian women can read this account of Mary and desire to emulate her sacrificial service. In John 12:3 we read another account of this occasion:

> Then Mary took a pound of very costly oil of spikenard, anointed the feet of Jesus, and wiped His feet with her hair. And the house was filled with the fragrance of the oil.

"The house was filled with the fragrance of the oil." If only this could be said of our service! Whether in the home, the neighborhood, or the church — wherever we may work, if we do all for "love of Him" the devotion will fill the place and God will be glorified.

This was an extravagant display of devotion on Mary's part, but she was praised for it. Let us do with our might what our hands find to do. "And whatever you do, do it heartily, as to the Lord and not to men, knowing that from the Lord you will receive the reward of the inheritance, for you serve the Lord Christ" (Colossians 3:23,24).

In my book *Cups Running Over*, I wrote the following story:

> Julia (our daughter) was practicing her piano lessons. "Its a joy to hear her," I thought. "She works so hard at it, and she really seems to enjoy it. Her fingers seem to fly over the keys, and there is a quality of love and devotion in that playing."
>
> I wish I could pour forth that quality of devotion in all the daily tasks that I perform. Sometimes my tasks seem never-ending, and they all have to be performed over and over again, day after day. I am sure I do not perform them with the enthusiasm I should.
>
> As Julia plays, the whole music, created by her skill and devotion seems to fill the house. Sometimes she vocalizes her feelings, like the day she exclaimed extravagantly, "Mother, I just couldn't stop playing. I just wanted to go on and on!"
>
> How I wish I could carry some of this exuberance and enthusiasm into my own daily acts of service. If I could just put the love and devotion that Julia puts into her music, I believe it would be felt by the entire family.

A Time for Every Purpose

Ecclesiastes 3:17 reads this way:

> "For there shall be a time for every purpose and for every work."

Are you guilty of saying, "When I have time . . . ?" How often do we procrastinate and put off a loving deed because we expect to have more time later. Alas, there is never *more* time!

All the time we have is right now — today. It is true that we can never do all that we would like to do today — many things have to be put off until tomorrow — but why do we put off doing the kind things, the things that bless and help another? Why do we think that another time or day will be more appropriate than this day?

When I Have Time

When I have time, so many things I'll do
To make life happier and much more fair
For those whose lives are crowded now with care
I'll help to lift them from their low despair
When I have time.

When I have time, the friend I love so well
Shall know no more these weary toiling ways;
I'll lead her feet in pleasant paths always,
And cheer her heart with words of sweetest praise
When I have time.

Now is the time! Ah, friend, no longer wait
To scatter loving smiles and words of cheer
To those around whose lives are now so drear,
They may not meet you in the coming year
Now is the time!

— Author Unknown

Our heavenly Father has provided plenty of time for us to do those things which will bless the lives of others. But time runs out for all of us. We need to do what we can this very day.

> But this I say: He who sows sparingly will also reap sparingly, and he who sows bountifully will also reap bountifully. So let each one give as he purposes in his heart, not grudgingly or of necessity; for God loves a cheerful giver. And God is able to make all grace abound toward you, that you, always having all sufficiency in all things, have an abundance for every good work (2 Corinthians 9:6-8).

The Seeds We Sow

The seeds we sow within our life
Can bring us joy — can bring us strife,
For always we shall find tis true
What you send out comes back to you,
You reap it all — the good — the bad
The happy times or those quite sad.

The seeds we sow we ever find
Should be just those so sweet and kind,
For jealousy must not be known
Nor seeds of hate or envy sown,
If peace and gladness you would seek
Then kindly thoughts your heart must keep.

The harvest time will surely come
As seeds mature within life's sun,
And every one you plant and tend
Can bring a dear and lasting friend,
And as we live we'll ever know
We reap rewards from seeds we sow.

— Garnett Ann Schultz

Leftovers

I am reminded of the words of a prayer that our son Scott worded one time just before the contribution was taken:

> Dear Father, You have promised us in Your Word that if we seek Your Kingdom, You will give us all we need. Help us in our giving. Help us to really sacrifice and not give just what is left over. In Jesus' Name, Amen.

This really touched my heart, for I wonder how many times my servce has been rendered from the leftovers in my life.

Leftovers

Leftovers are such humble things,
  We would not serve to a guest
And yet we serve them to our Lord
  Who deserves the very best.
We give to Him leftover time,
  Stray minutes here and there.
Leftover cash we give to Him,
  Such few coins as we can spare.
We give our youth into the world,
  To hatred, lust and strife;
Then in declining years we give
  To Him the remnant of our life.

— Author Unknown

Serve God Acceptably

> Therefore by Him let us continually offer the sacrifice of praise to God, that is, the fruit of our lips, giving thanks to His name. But do not forget to do good and to share, for with such sacrifices God is well pleased (Hebrews 13:15,16).

In order for any of us to serve God acceptably, we must present our bodies (our total being) a living sacrifice; one that is not conformed to this world, but one that has been renewed in our minds. The writer of Hebrews also gives the servant of God some guidelines to follow:

> Therefore, since we are receiving a kingdom which cannot be shaken, let us have grace, by which we may serve God acceptably, with reverence and godly fear (Hebrews 12:28).

There are four aspects of this verse which we would do well to incorporate into our thinking concerning the servant's spirit:

1. We are receiving a kingdom which cannot be shaken. (The gates of hell shall never prevail against it.)
2. We are given the free gift of grace which enables us to serve. (His grace is sufficient).

3. We are to serve God acceptably.
   (From the greek word DEKTOS meaning a person or thing who has been regarded favorably).
4. We are to serve with reverence and godly fear.
   (Mingled fear and love directed toward our God).

This godly reverence which we are to manifest toward God will keep us from anxieties and worry. Worry is a common occurrence among those who lack a complete trust in God. Worry keeps us from attempting many good deeds out of fear that our gifts will be spurned or rejected. We all fear rejection on the part of others.

Why be handicapped by fear? God has promised: "Lo, I am with you and will be in you." This causes us to boldly say:

> The Lord is my helper;
> I will not fear.
> What can man do to me? (Hebrews 13:6).

Our own strengths and abilities will get us nowhere. Only in God's power and strength can any of us give ourselves away in service. What a privilege it is to have Christ motivate and direct us. We need never have to be petrified with fear and self doubt again. Christ will do His work through us. We need to surrender our egos and let Him have His way with us.

Someone has said, "You may never get hurt if you don't stick your neck out, but you will also probably never do anything of value!"

I also like the statement which Albert Schweitzer has made:

> Of this I am certain.
> The only ones among you who
> will be truly happy are those
> who have sought and found
> how to serve.

Our Greatest Service

The greatest service we can do for anyone is to bring him into a saving relationship with the Lord Jesus. Soul winning calls for the highest sacrifice on our parts. Yet there is nothing which holds a more satisfying reward. The soul winner must have the servant's spirit.

For though I am free from all men, I have made myself a servant to all, that I might win the more; (1 Corinthians 9:19).

Where do we begin? I believe with all my heart that we must begin in the *home*. Once we have taken care of the needs there, we can and must extend ourselves further. We must not hide behind the cloak of motherhood or being a housewife.

Deborah, the prophetess and judge, said in her battle song: "I, Deborah, arose a mother in Israel." We as mothers in America must arise to defend the great and wonderful heritage of our country — that of keeping our nation intact for Christ Jesus. No nation is greater than the homes in that nation.

Christ has no hands but our hands to meet the needs of others today. He has no feet but our feet to carry the message of hope and grace. He has no mouth but our mouths to tell the "good news" that Jesus saves. Sometimes we go fishing. Eagerly watching the water for any little ripples, we sit there with excitement in our hearts. We know that where we see ripples, there may be hope of a catch.

God is always with us, helping and giving us strength; we need never serve Him alone. We frustrate the grace of God when we do not allow Him to work through us. "I must work the works of Him that sent Me while it is day; the night is coming when no one can work" (John 9:4).

All of us have friends who are outside the will of God. We need to do what we can to lead that person into the Father's will.

My Friend?

My friend, I stand in the judgement now
And feel that you're to blame some how.
On earth I walked with you day by day,
And never did you point the way.

You knew the Lord in truth and glory,
But never did you tell the story.
My knowledge then was very dim,
You could have led me safe to Him.

Tho' we lived together on the earth,
You never told me of the second birth;
And now I stand this day condemned,
Because you failed to mention Him.

You taught me many things, that's true;
I called you "friend" and trusted you.
But I learn now that it's too late;
You could have kept me from this fate.

We walked by day and talked by night,
And yet you showed me not the light.
You let me live, and love, and die,
You knew I'd never live on High.

Yes, I called you "friend" in life,
And trusted you through joy and strife,
And yet, on coming to this end,
I cannot, now, call you "My friend!"

— Author Unknown

Stretched Out Hands

In the narrative of the worthy woman as told in Proverbs 31:20, Solomon us that a woman has so much love to give that it cannot possibly stop with her family. Her hands are continually stretched out to anyone in need.

"She extends her hand to the poor; and she stretches out her hands to the needy." It is good to do as much as we can for those who are less fortunate than we — it is far more helpful to reach a needy person. Who is more needful than the person without Christ Jesus?

When we look about us and see the needs of people, we realize the solution to all their problems is found in Christ. We can build up their hopes in Christ, establish their faithfulness and bring them to obedience to Christ's will.

Tell of His Salvation

In Mark the 5th chapter, we are told that Jesus had just healed a man who had an unclean spirit. Afterwards the man pleaded with Jesus to allow him to be with Him.

> However, Jesus did not permit him, but said to him, "Go home to your friends, and tell them what great things the Lord has done for you, and how he has had compassion on you" (Mark 5:19).

The Lord gave that man some wonderful advice. In effect, he was saying, "The best way you can serve me is to go home and tell your friends what I have done for you — tell *them* about my compassion and love."

This holds true for any of us. Once we have experienced the great love and compassion of our Savior, we need to share it with loved ones at home, both family and friends and others who will listen.

Paul says much the same thing in Philippians 2:1 and 2:

> Therefore if there is any consolation in Christ, if any comfort of love, if any fellowship of the Spirit, if any affection and mercy, fulfill my joy by being like-minded, having the same love, being of one accord, of one mind.

If God has been merciful to us as sinners, and has "delivered up from the power of darkness and translated us into the kingdom of the son of His love" (Colossians 1:13), how much more should we "tell of His salvation from day to day" (1 Chronicles 16:23).

What Would He Say?

If He should come today
And find my hands so full
Of future plans, however fair,
In which my Savior has no share,
What would He say?

If He should come today
And find my love so cold,
My faith so very weak and dim
I had not even looked for Him,
What would He say?

If He should come today
And find I had not told
One soul about my heavenly Friend
Whose blessings all my way attend,
What would He say?

> If He should come today
> Would I be glad — quite glad?
> Remembering He had died for all
> And none, through me, had heard His call
> What would He say?
>
> — Author Unknown

A Burning Fire

When Jesus becomes the one "in whom we live and move and have our being," we will not be able to refrain from telling others about Him. In the 4th chapter of Acts, we are told that Peter and John were threatened with yet another prison sentence if they spoke or taught anymore in the name of Jesus.

Peter and John could not be threatened. They answered the authorities in this way:

> Whether it is right in the sight of God to listen to you more than to God, you judge. For we cannot but speak the things which we have seen and heard (Acts 4:19,20).

The people paid attention and listened to Peter and John because "they realized that they had been with Jesus" (Acts 4:13).

People will be able to tell whether we have been with Jesus or not, and they will listen to us or tune us out according to how much they see Jesus in us. We must tell others of His saving grace.

In the 20th chapter of Jeremiah we are told that this great prophet was about to give up because he had been treated with much cruelty. Yet in his heart he could not do it. This is his great statement:

> Then I said, "I will not make mention of Him,
> Nor speak anymore in His name."
> But His word was in my heart like a burning fire
> Shut up in my bones;
> I was weary of holding it back,
> And I could Not (Jeremiah 20:9).

Talk about sacrifice! Jeremiah was willing to be thrown into pit after pit; even to be slain for His name's sake. There was just one thing he could not do. He could not be quiet about the Lord. He proclaimed boldly:

> "But the Lord is with me as a mighty, awesome one" (Jeremiah 20:11).

With that kind of faith, Jeremiah was determined to proclaim His name. Neither persecution or death would keep him from it.

Ladies, let's not be weary of forbearing any longer. Let's not keep this burning fire containing the message of Christ shut up in our bones any longer. Let us speak out and warm the hearts of all those around us, beginning in our very own homes!

Psalm 107:2 thunders forth with a message we should never forget:

> "Let the redeemed of the Lord say so!"

CHAPTER FIVE

SOMETHING TO THINK ABOUT TODAY

1. Little service is accomplished without _____.
2. What is perhaps the hardest part of service?
3. What would you say is one of our biggest problems in service?
4. When we are frightened at the prospect of involvement, what would be a good verse for us to remember and practice?
   "_____ _____ _____ _____ ___ _____."
5. 2 Timothy 1:7 tells us that God has not given us a spirit of fear (or timidity). Name three qualities He has given us. _____, _____ and __ _____ _____.
6. Under the sub head **Biblical Truths** are listed three verses desirable for memorization. As you memorize these verses this week, consider why it is easier to believe and say these verses, than it is to practice them.
7. We need to develop an _____ _____ toward our Lord. We love Him best by _____ _____ to His other children.
8. Any service that we do for other people should cost us something in _____ _____.
9. When Mary anointed the feet of Jesus and wiped His feet with her hair, the whole house was filled with _____ _____ ____ _____ _____.
10. Why do we procrastinate and put off many loving deeds?
11. Discuss the principle of reaping and sowing as found in 2 Corinthians 9:6-8.
12. Discuss the four aspects found in Hebrews 12:28.
13. _____ keeps us from attempting many good deeds out of _____ our gifts will be _____ and _____.
14. What is the greatest service we can do for anyone?
15. Where does soul winning begin?
16. Why did the people pay attention and listen to Peter and John? What lesson can we learn from this?
17. What one thing could Jeremiah not do?
18. Have you ever pondered on the statement found in Psalm 107:2? Write it down here _____.
    The question you and I must ask is: "Do we really believe this verse? Why do we not act upon it then?"

CHAPTER SIX

A COOPERATIVE SPIRIT

The Family of God

It is wonderful to be a Christian, serving in the family of God. One of our common bonds is the ability to recognize our dependence on God to unify all our efforts in service.

Paul encouraged the Corinthian brethren by clarifying their position:

> I planted, Apollos watered, but God gave the increase. So then neither he who plants is anything, nor he who waters, but God who gives the increase. Now he who plants and he who waters are one, and each one will receive his own reward according to his own labor.
>
> For we are God's fellow workers; you are God's field, you are God's building. According to the grace of God which was given to me, as a wise master builder I have laid the foundation, and another builds on it. But let each one take heed how he builds on it (1 Corinthians 3:6-10).

Special Things

In other words, each does her own *special thing* in building the body of Christ. Each one will receive her own special reward. The important thing to remember is that "we are God's fellow workers." God gives the increase, while asking us to do the planting and the watering. Paul referred to us as "workers together with Him" (2 Corinthians 6:1).

Special Things

God gives each one some special thing to do
    To further His great kingdom on the earth.
What is within your hand the long day through
    To shape into some vital thing of worth
For God's own glory and for your soul's good,
    For the good of others as you travel on?
What craft, what splendid art is yours that would
    Make life the richer before day is done?

Perhaps it may be but the gentle art
    Of being kind to others in their need,
A faculty for easing some hurt heart
    Or eyes to see or listening ears to heed
The constant cry for help from land to land,
    What is it, O comrade, in your hand?

Many Members in the One Body

In the 12th chapter of 1 Corinthians, Paul describes the worth and value of each Christian. He tells them that every member has been given a gift (or talent). Each one's gift is different, yet entrusted to us by the same Spirit (verse 4).

He goes on to say that there are different ways to serve God, "but it is the same God who works all in all" (verse 6).

God, who knows our hearts, gives us different talents and urges us to develop and use them — serving God with one spirit and mind. The outcome of this service is that all will be blessed, all will be encouraged and built up.

Grace Bestows Different Gifts

When Paul wrote to the brethren at Rome, he had this to say:

> So in Christ we who are many form one body, and each member belongs to all the others. We have different gifts, according to the grace given us. If a man's gift is prophesying, let him use it in proportion to his faith. If it is serving, let him serve; if it is teaching, let him teach; if it is encouraging, let him encourage; if it is contributing to the needs of others, let him give generously;

if it is leadership, let him govern diligently; if it is showing mercy, let him do it cheerfully (Romans 12:5-8). NIV

Through God's wonderful grace, each one of us is enabled to serve in some capacity. God has a great work for each one of us to do. "Now you are the body of Christ, and each one of you is a part of it" (1 Corinthians 12:27). No service for God is too small — God accepts even the smallest deed with love and honor.

This Is My Church

It is composed of people like me,
It will bring other people into its worship
   and fellowship if I bring them.
It will be a church of loyalty and love,
   of fearlessness and faith,
   and a church of a noble spirit —
   if I, who make it what it is,
   am filled with these.
Therefore, with the help of God,
   I shall dedicate myself
   to the task of being all the things
   that I want my church to be.

— Author Unknown

Building Talents

It is important that each of us discover our unique gifts and talents. Most of us are not born with natural abilities. They must be cultivated along the way.

For the most part, it is usually the thing which we enjoy doing most which determines our natural gifts. We can become selfish about our natural gifts but gifts should never be hoarded or used for our own satisfaction.

Someone has said, "The believer's talents are not to be laid up for self, but laid out in service."

When a talent is hoarded, we become like the man who was given one talent and then went and buried it.

> Then he who had received the one talent came
> and said, "Lord, I knew you to be a hard man,

reaping where you have not sown, and gathering where you have not scattered seed. And I was afraid, and went and hid your talent in the ground. Look, there you have what is yours."

But his lord answered and said to him, "You wicked and lazy servant, you knew that I reap where I have not sown, and gather here I have not scattered seed. Therefore you ought to have deposited my money with the bankers, and at my coming I would have received back my own with interest."

Therefore take the talent from him, and give it to him who has ten talents. For to everyone who has, more will be given, and he will have abundance; but from him who does not have, even what he has will be taken away.

And cast the unprofitable servant into the outer darkness. There will be weeping and gnashing of teeth (Matthew 25:24-30).

One Talent

In a napkin smooth and white, hidden from all mortal sight,
  My one talent lies tonight.
Mine to hoard, or mine to use; mine to keep or mine to lose,
  May I not do what I choose?

Ah! The gift was only lent, with the Giver's known intent
  That it should be wisely spent.
And I know He will demand every farthing from my hand,
  When I in His presence stand.

What will be my grief and shame when I hear my humble name
  And cannot repay His claim!
One poor talent — nothing more — all the years that have gone o'er
  Have not added to the store.

Some will double what they hold; others add to it tenfold
  And pay back the shining gold.
Would that I had toiled like them, all my sloth I now condemn;
  Guilty fears my soul overwhelm.

Lord, oh teach me what to do; make me faithful, make me true,
  And that sacred trust renew.
Help me, ere too late it be, something yet to do for Thee,
  Thou who hast done all for me.

— Author Unknown

Unprofitable Servants

Let us never be unprofitable servants (Luke 17:10) whose lights are hidden under baskets. Let us light lamps and place them upon lamp stands for all the house to see (Matthew 5:15). All talents, abilities and capabilities are *gifts* from God. They should be used to glorify our Father in heaven. We need to place ourselves in positions of service where our talents and gifts can be utilized best.

Talents

If you are an artist
  Paint for the Lord,

If you are a sculpturer
  Sculpture for the Lord,

If you are a seamstress
  Sew for the Lord,

If you are a singer
  Sing for the Lord,

If you are a teacher
  Teach for the Lord,

If you are a mother
  Raise children for the Lord,

If you are a writer,
  Write for the Lord.

Whatever you do in word or deed
  Do all in the name of the
    Lord!

— Judy Miller

Whatever you do well, do it for Jesus! I would like to encourage more of you to *write* for the Lord. If you do not know how to go about doing this, I would suggest you simply start writing. Begin with a notebook or journal in which you write down your thoughts, feelings and ideas about what God is doing in your daily life. This is the way I began my writing.

I have kept an on-going daily journal for 20 years. I wish I had started my recordings sooner. In my journal I write down what I have learned that day about the Lord, circumstances, the people who have gone in and out of my day, the conversations with my family, friends and students. I record the lessons that I have learned which have made me a better person and servant, also my longings, prayers and dreams. These things need to be shared with others.

Stewards of His Gifts

Peter tells us how to use our gifts in 1 Peter 4:10 and 11:

> As each one has received a gift, minister it to one another, as good stewards of the manifold grace of God. If anyone speaks, let him speak as the oracles of God. If anyone ministers, let him do it as with the ability which God supplies, that in all things God may be glorified through Jesus Christ . . .

Wouldn't it be wonderful if we could realize the truth and beauty of this statement? God has appointed us as stewards of his many faceted grace! We are to take our gifts and minister (serve) one another with them.

When our gifts are freely given, we demonstrate the grace of God in a marvelous way. God supplies the ability; we need not be concerned with that part of our service. So often we fret and stew about our abilities or lack of them. God will take care of your stewardship. All we need do is use them for Him, to bring glory to His name.

John Ruskin once said, "The constant duty of every man is to use his own special gifts, and to strengthen them for the help of others."

The manifold grace of God means that God has so much grace to give; once we have received this grace we are to share that same grace with others.

Isn't it wonderful to know that while we are serving others, God can be glorified through that service? We do not serve so that we can be recognized for our abilities. We do not *show off* our talents and gifts, but we *give* our abilities away freely, that God may be gloried and exalted.

Areas of Service

In all probability God will show us areas of service that we never dreamed possible. God always surprises the heart that dreams, yearns, reaches for and develops itself.

Remember how Moses responded to the call of God to lead His people out of Egypt? First of all, he was quite startled that God should call one as lowly and untalented as he. He immediately questioned God:

> Who am I that I should go to Pharaoh, and that I should bring the children of Israel out of Egypt? (Exodus 3:11).

God simply replied:

> I will certainly be with you (Verse 12).

Following this interaction, God imposed on Moses several signs that would help the people believe. Moses was troubled. Even after God had demonstrated His power in the most dynamic ways, Moses was still obsessed with the one inadequacy he felt would keep him from accepting God's commission.

> O my Lord, I am not eloquent neither before nor since You have spoken to Your servant; but I am slow of speech and slow of tongue (Exodus 4:10).

The Lord said to him:

> Who has made man's mouth? Or who makes the mute, the deaf, the seeing, or the blind? Have not I, the Lord? Now, therefore, go, and I will be with your mouth and teach you what you shall say (verses 11 and 12).

For Moses, this was not enough. He was yet to build that powerful, unswerving trust and faith which would cause the writer of Hebrews to say:

> And Moses indeed was faithful in all His house as a servant, for a testimony of those things which should be spoken afterward (Hebrews 3:5).

Meanwhile, Moses backed away and said what you and I are always saying, "Just send anyone but me!" God was not about to give up on Moses. His anger was really provoked by now. Nevertheless, Aaron became His spokesman . . . and little by little, Moses gained enough confidence to be God's bold spokesman himself.

Though God relented and allowed Aaron to be His primary speaker awhile it was Moses He wanted, and Moses He finally *got*.

Fellowship of Christian Servants

God has made us so that we feel especially close to certain people. We have many friends, but brothers and sisters in Christ usually care about one another more than most. Paul refers to this divine relationship as "the household of God" or "the household of faith." We are given precious assurance from Paul's statement in Ephesians 2:19:

> Now, therefore, you are no longer strangers and foreigners, but fellow citizens with the saints and members of the household of God.

We are also told in Galatians 6:9 and 10:

> And let us not grow weary while doing good, for in due season we shall reap if we do not lose heart. Therefore, as we have opportunity, let us do good to all, especially to those who are of the household of faith.

It is so easy for us to "grow weary" in serving others. Time and again, we "lose heart" because nothing seems to come from our service. The good accomplished goes unseen . . . seldom do we receive any encouragement. This should not deter us — we serve because Jesus served, and because He has asked us to become like Him. "In due season" we shall be rewarded, which calls for all the patience we can muster.

We need to encourage each other in the "household of faith." The Hebrew writer tells us: "And let us consider one another in order to stir up love and good works" (Hebrews 10:24).

Any time we have an opportunity in the family of God, we are to encourage, stir one another up, and do good. The members of God's household are the dearest and closest to us on earth. We are "to do good to all, especially to those of the household of faith."

Christians have a different family relationship — we have the privilege of being a part of two families — not just one. In the Church of Christ, we are a spiritual family; members of a community — the Christian community. We have God as our Father. We are His beloved children, honoring Him as King and Savior.

I believe we have not properly appreciated the fellowship that takes place in the church. The sweet, warm, abiding friendship that we experience with one another in the Christian family is a true gift of love and grace and we should accept it as such and be grateful.

In the world, we often experience a fragmentation that leaves us lonely and separated from our fellow beings. But in the church, we find a family — "the household of faith." First Corinthians 12:12 points out that we live in a relationship with every other member in the family. This is called *koinonia* or fellowship. I thought it would be interesting to look up the word "fellowship" in the dictionary. A brief meaning is given: "A group of people with the same interests." But look how different the description reads in the Bible dictionary:

> "That heavenly love which fills or should fill the
> heart of believers for one another and for God."

In the Scriptures we have a word that describes this fellowship. It is the Greek word "agape" which means godly love. This fellowship and love is deeper and more satisfying than any earthly love.

Wherever I travel, whenever I am called upon to share the Christian message with my sisters in Christ, one significant fact stands out. There is a close-knit bond of love and fellowship among true believers that exists in no other area of society. It is a kinship of like precious faith that draws us together in close relationship. We all belong to the redeemed family of God.

Even though we may be complete strangers, when a child of God meets another child of God, we feel a oneness and genuine warmth. We have much in common — we belong. The closeness we feel is not only because we share similar experiences; but because the same Father, the same Holy Spirit, and the same Jesus Christ indwells us all. We are spiritual relatives — sisters in the Lord. God is our Father and we are His children. This tie is far stronger than any earthly tie can possibly be. That is why we are told in Galatians 6:2 to "bear one another's burdens."

It is a relationship that will last for eternity. Blessed be the tie that binds our hearts together in Christian love and service.

The Church — The Called Out Ones

The word church comes from the Greek word *ekklesia* meaning "The called out ones." It comes from *ek* which means "out of" and *klesis* which means "a calling." It is also described as "the church, which is His body" in Ephesians 1:23. Christians are also referred to as "the elect of God" in Colossians 3:12-15. This passage goes on to describe how we are to live as "the called out ones," "the elect," and "the one body."

> Therefore, as the elect of God, holy and beloved, put on tender mercies, kindness, humbleness of mind, meekness, long-suffering; bearing with one another and forgiving one another, if anyone has a complaint against another; even as Christ forgave you, so you also must do. But above all these things put on love, which is the bond of perfection. And let the peace of God rule in your hearts, *to which also you were called in one body;* and be thankful. (Italics mine).

As "called out ones" we need to remember we were called out of the world into God's kingdom. We are called to a life of service in the name of Jesus Christ.

God is faithful, who knows the hearts of all men, especially those of the household of faith. He knows we could never be happy if there was no one to serve. As God's "called out ones" let us be like servants who obey their earthly masters, "not with eyeservice, as menpleasers, but in sincerity of heart, fearing God" (Colossians 3:22).

Prayer Life of Christians

One of the greatest services we can render toward our fellow Christians is to pray for them. Paul recognized this fact when he wrote to the church at Phillipi:

> I thank my God upon every remembrance of you, always in every prayer of mine making request for you all with joy, for your fellowship in the gospel from the first day until now, being confident of this very thing, that He who has begun a good work in you will complete it until the day of Jesus Christ (Philippians 1:3-6).

How deep the prayer life of the church should be. Praying with and for one another is one of the greatest joys in the kingdom. How often we need to hold each other up in prayer in definite, specific ways. Why is it so hard to look at some one and say, "I'll pray for you," or "I know you've been having difficulties lately, and I've been praying for you."

Why is it so hard to ask, "Will you pray for me?"

One of the most rewarding blessings that has come out of our Ladies' Bible classes in recent months has been the participation of our Ladies in praying for one another. We draw names in our Wednesday night class, and for three months we are to pray for this sister in specific ways.

How comforting to know that my sister is praying for me. How uplifting it is for me to remember her in prayer also.

Several years ago, a sister in my class and I were engaged in conversation. "How is your back trouble?" I asked. "Oh, much improved," she related. "I know why," I told her. "Keep it up, I need it," she stated. Passing me one day as I entered the worship service, she whispered, "Pease pray for my son." That was all. No need to say anything else.

Oh, how we need to hold each other up in prayer.

At one time, my prayer sister's name was Mary. I wrote this poem for her:

The Gift Of Praying

Here I am, Mary.
Ready and anxious
To begin this adventure
In prayer with you.

I don't know you very well, Mary
You don't know me either.
But there is One who knows
Everything there is to know
About both of us.

It's an exciting moment, Mary
To think about the potential
And possibilities we hold
Within the confines of our hearts
Through prayer.

I need your prayers, Mary
Do you need mine?
I have some needs, Mary
Do you want to know
What they are?
Will you tell me your needs?
I really want to know.

There are days so bursting
With joy and peace and love
I simply have to tell someone
about them,
Would you care to be the one?

There are days I'm so worried
And depressed and down
If I knew you were praying for me
I wouldn't feel so sad.

It's strange this power
We receive through prayer.
I think the Father
Must have known we needed Him
And needed each other
So He taught us how to pray.

It's true we can only give
Part of ourselves to each other
When He gave *all* of Himself.
But don't you think
That through this partial giving
We'll find more of *Him*
Than we've ever known before?

> I need to grow, Mary
> Do you feel this way too?
> I need to stretch my spirit.
> I know I can best do this
> By helping you to stretch
> Your spirit too.
>
> Do you know what I mean?
> We have received a gift, you and me.
> The gift of praying,
> You for me, and I for you.
> Shall we take this gift
> Each together
> And give it back to God?

Limitations in the Church

Far too much time has been spent in declaring women's limitations in the church. I would briefly like to mention these restrictions, then move on to the services a woman may perform in the church.

1. A woman must be under the authority of her husband (1 Corinthians 11:3).
2. A woman may not be an elder. "A bishop then must be blameless, the husband of one wife" (1 Timothy 3:2).
3. Women are not allowed to have authority over the men in the affairs of the church. "For God is not the author of confusion but of peace, as in all the churches of the saints. Let your women keep silence in the churches, for they are not permitted to speak; but they are to be submissive, as the law also says (1 Corinthians 14:33-34). "Let a woman learn in silence with all submission. And I do not permit a woman to teach or to have authority over a man, but to be in silence" (1 Timothy 2:11,12).

These scriptures plainly reveal the will of God. Men and women have always found their highest happiness within the sweet will of God. How precious are His statutes, and His judgements toward the children of men.

Acts of Service for Women

The following are a few of the things that a Christian woman can and must do for the Lord:

1. Train and teach the younger women (Titus 2:4).
2. Labor with ministers of the gospel of Christ (Philippians 4:3).
3. Open your home to ministers of the gospel as Lydia did (Acts 16:15).
4. Be a servant of the church like Phoebe (Romans 16:1 and 2).
5. Be full of good works and alms-deeds as Dorcus (Acts 9:36-43).
6. Open your home for a prayer meeting like Mary (Acts 12:12-17).
7. Be a personal worker for the Lord as was Priscilla (Acts 18:26).
8. Do what you can with whatever ability God has given you. "She has done what she could" (Mark 14:8).
9. Do much benevolent work (1 Timothy 2:10).
10. Pray often in private, not aloud in the assembly (Colossians 4:2).
11. Study and know God through your Bible, and share this knowledge with others (2 Timothy 2:15).
12. Be hospitable (Romans 12:13).
13. Participate in teaching Bible Correspondence courses (World Bible School is one of the best ways of spreading the Word).
14. Other good works:
    a. Write notes to sick, newcomers, new parents, bereaved, etc;
    b. Provide transportation to services for those who need it.
    c. Prepare food for shut-ins, bereaved, sick, etc;
    d. Visit weak members, visitors to service, new members, etc;
    e. Sing at funerals.
    f. Help encourage newlyweds and parents (showers).
    g. Help young converts when they are baptized.
    h. Have new converts into your home. Encourage them in every possible way.

Many times we do not know where and how to serve, but God's will is good, acceptable and perfect. Let us base all our decisions on where and how to serve by depending upon His perfect will.

One important thing we need to remember is to learn when to say "yes" graciously, and when to say "no" firmly. So many times we are caught up in a pursuit of activities which actually hinder our service. We are doing far too many things. It would be better to concentrate on doing one thing well.

Sometimes we feel as if we are going in a hundred different directions at one time. I read about one woman who said that she felt like a "piece of pie which had to be sliced six ways to serve ten different people."

No one woman needs to spread herself that thin, especially the young woman with small children. When young children are in the home, their needs should come first before all else.

In summation, let us remember that not everyone serves God in the same way and manner. All of us have differing abilities and talents. "Do not neglect the gift that is in you," admonished Paul to Timothy his son in the faith. Let us learn from this.

We are to develop the gift that is in us, not someone else's gift. We can't borrow another's gifts. God gave us our own set. Whether they are few or many, what we do with them is our gift to God.

CHAPTER SIX

SOMETHING TO THINK ABOUT TODAY

1. Name one of our common bonds in the church?
2. When we as Christians plant and water, what does God promise on His part?
3. God knows our _____, gives _____ _____, and urges us to _____ and _____ them, serving God with one _____ and _____.
4. Discuss the power of God's grace in Christian service.
5. True or false?
   A. We are born with natural abilities.
   B. Usually the thing we enjoy doing most determines our natural gifts.
   C. Our gifts should be used entirely for our own satisfaction.
   D. All talents, abilities and capabilities are gifts from God.
   E. They should be used to glorify our heavenly Father.
   F. There is no need to share our gifts. Just enjoy them.
6. Turn to 1 Peter 4:10 and 11, and examine every facet of this passage. In what way does this verse explain the grace of God?
7. What does the expression "the manifold grace of God" mean?
8. What was Moses' response to God's call? How does his response relate to us?
9. Name some ways we can "lose heart" in Christian service?
10. In the Church of Christ, we are a _____ _____. We are His _____ _____.
11. What is the beautiful Greek word for "fellowship?" What is the Bible dictionary meaning of fellowship?
12. Why is the church referred to as the "called out" ones? From what Greek word is this description derived?
13. Why is it so hard to ask, "Will you pray for me?"
14. Is praying for others an act of Christian service? Why?
15. Name three biblical restrictions placed upon a woman's service.
16. Look at each of the suggested Scriptures for acts of service listed in this chapter. Give a three minute talk on each one.
17. Why is it so important to learn to say "yes" graciously, and "no" firmly?

CHAPTER 7

A DEVOTIONAL SPIRIT

Reverence and Godly Fear

We have studied in Hebrews 12:28 that we are to serve God with reverence and godly fear. The biblical concept of reverence includes respect, awe, fear and honor.

Before any act of genuine service takes place, we must revere His holy name. Joshua told the Israelites:

> Now therefore, fear the Lord, serve Him in sincerity and in truth, and put away the gods which your fathers served on the other side of the River and in Egypt. Serve the Lord! And if it seems evil to you to serve the Lord, choose for yourselves this day whom you will serve . . . But as for me and my house, we will serve the Lord (Joshua 24:14 and 15).

Joshua, along with all his house chose to serve Jehovah God. Godly fear, along with love motivates us to service. We should be careful lest a spirit of callousness and foolishness slip in. All service should be done for His name's honor and glory.

In Isaiah the 6th chapter, we read about Isaiah visualizing the Lord high and lifted up. The Lord was sitting on a throne, and above His throne stood seraphim. One cried to another and said:

> Holy, holy, holy is the Lord of hosts;
> The whole earth is full of His glory!

One of the seraphim flew to Isaiah and touched his mouth with a live coal. After this, Isaiah heard the voice of the Lord saying:

> Whom shall I send,
> And who will go for us?

Isaiah cried out: "Here am I! Send me."

Isaiah was ready to go after he had seen the Lord high and lifted up. It is wonderful to seek the Father's face, to praise Him with fervent love, then go out in the strength of the Lord.

> In the fear of the Lord there is strong confidence,
> And His children will have a place of refuge
> The fear of the Lord is a fountain of life . . .
> (Proverbs 14:26,27).

Man's relationship to God and others can be illustrated by a fountain with an upper and lower basin. The upper basin represents our love to God. Its overflow into the lower basin is our love for others. Our love for others has its origin in our love for God.
— Author Unknown

Balanced Devotion

The servant's spirit is a characteristic all Christian women should desire. It is true for the most part that we are constantly being called upon to help and serve others. Someone has written:

> To feel, to love, to suffer, to give, will always be
> the text of the life of a woman.

This being the case, how can a woman continually be strong and giving? Many requests come, begging for her time, energy and strength. How can she keep from falling under such a load of demands?

It takes a great deal out of a woman when she is asked over and over to give herself away. The constant demands on a wife, mother, homemaker and Christian servant are numerous. The strain on her can be debilitating if she does not balance her devotion with discretion and reason.

The Virtuous Woman

Let us take a look at the busy, demanding schedule of the virtuous woman as detailed in Proverbs 31:

She seeks wool and flax
She willingly works with her hands
She brings her food from afar
She rises while it is yet night
She provides food for her household
She gives a portion to her maid servants
She considers a field and keeps it
She plants a vineyard
She perceives that her merchandise is good
She stretches out her hands to the distaff
She reaches out her hands to the needy
She clothes her family with scarlet
She makes tapestry for herself
She makes it possible for her husband to be known in the gates
She makes linen garments and sells them
She supplies sashes for the merchants
She opens her mouth with wisdom
She speaks only kind words
She watches over her household
She spends no time in idleness.

Help! If I had to do all that, I'd faint before 10 o'clock in the morning!

This is a picture of a completely devoted woman who *loved* to serve. Notice, with one exception, she was serving others. The one exception was the sewing of garments for herself ... yet, this wasn't altogether selfish, for it probably saved her husband a great deal of money, which is a *real* service.

How was it possible for this woman to accomplish so much, and this so routinely, day by day? The secret is found in two verses:

> She girds herself with strength, and strengthens her arms (verse 17).

> But a woman who fears the Lord, she shall be praised (verse 30).

What an excellent combination!

1. She girded herself with strength (notice, she took definite action to do this.)
2. She feared the Lord.

Christian women are constantly giving of themselves; pouring their love on other people. As a result, sometimes we find ourselves feeling drained of all stamina and strength.

We can learn a lot from this excellent woman portrayed so vividly in Proverbs 31. Instead of feeling intimidated by this energetic, accomplished woman, we can pause and consider the source of this woman's strength.

Because this woman "whose worth is far above rubies" feared the Lord and was praised for it, we can only conclude that the way she girded herself with strength was from *above*.

I believe she also strengthened her body by eating good, wholesome food and by engaging in exercise. We know from verse 17 that she strengthened her arms. I also believe she strengthened her spirit by communicating with her Father above.

Both are important, but daily communication with God through prayer and Bible study is vital to a Christian woman's service and outreach. If any of us are to grow outwardly, we must first of all be enriched from within by God's love.

Robert A. Cook said: "Every day, spend enough time with your Lord to get something that spills out of your heart, because it is such a blessing. When you are full to the "spillover" point with blessings from God's Word, you will find far less difficulty in sharing it."

Replenishment

In her book *Gifts From The Sea,* Anne Morrow Lindburgh compares a woman to a water pitcher. She is expected to spill her gifts all around (a constant emptying of herself into the lives of others). Only in filling or replenishing herself with the Word of God can she find the necessary strength to continue pouring out her love and service. You cannot pour water from an *empty* pitcher.

It has to be filled! The way we are filled is through Bible study and prayer. I cannot emphasize enough the importance of a daily time with our Master. He refreshes and nurtures us. In so doing, our pitchers fill to the brim. Thus, we cannot help spilling out the contents to each other.

A candle doesn't stay lit forever. It burns down, doesn't it? We are to be used and burned up in the Lord's service. In order for us to be replenished, we must be nurtured ourselves.

The Torch

Lord, let me be the torch that springs to light
    And lives its life in one exultant flame,
One leap of living fire against the night,
    Dropping to darkness as it came.
For I have watched the smoldering of a soul
    Choked in the ashes that itself hath made,
Waiting the slow destruction of the whole,
    And turned from it, bewildered and afraid.
Light me with love, with all desire
    For that I may not reach, but let me burn
A little moment in pulsating fire.

— Author Unknown

We are partners with God. We are coworkers with Him. This helps us carry out God's plans in the world. Have you ever thought of helping God carry out His plans for the world? This knowledge causes us to respond: "Take all we have and use us for Your service, Lord."

The Will

Here is a good time to insert this principle: We do not give enough attention to the importance of the will in devotion and service. The will is the part of us placed deep within where God works, or where He is ignored and forgotten.

From this inner source (the indwelling spirit of God) we obtain the power, strength, wisdom and nourishment we need for service. This comes about when we are aware that God is at the hub of our lives. He is at the center of our wills. Everything else revolves around this focus.

When God is ignored, *our* will takes over and we have a difficult time with service. We don't see the urgency — we don't feel the need — we simply don't do it. As an opportunity presents itself, we cannot (or will not) summon enough motivation. This is because we haven't learned to submit our wills to the will of God.

A yielded sweet will harmonizes with God's will, yet we persist in holding onto our own way. It is certainly the most pleasurable. It pleases the flesh, and it doesn't take much guessing to determine *who* is behind this kind of mentality. Satan hates any form of service — he will use anything and everything to divert us from good intentions.

Satan comes as an angel of light. He connives and deceives us into believing our service wouldn't do much good anyway. Besides, we're too tired, too busy and too important. Let somebody else do that!

On and on he works with our minds. "They" might think we're imposing or interfering, etc. We need to heed the Scriptures which warn us not to be ignorant of Satan's devices. So often, this is exactly what happens. How else can you explain why more good works are not done, and more individuals helped?

Activity and Service

Let me insert quickly at this point, that it is quite possible for any of us to overdo or to overextend ourselves in unbalanced activities for the Lord. In many cases activity and service are not synonymous. There are any number of "good" Christian activities. They are fine — many times necessary. Yet *we cannot* participate in all of them. There has to be a happy, sane, sensible balance.

A mature Christian is one who has learned to balance activities and service on one hand, and the stewardship of mental, physical and emotional health on the other. There is only so much that one person can do.

It is very easy for us to equate "business" with "devotion." We feel a compulsion to "go-go-go," while all the time the "inward" man fails to be "renewed day by day" (2 Corinthians 4:16). As one writer states:

> "We are busy running the holy hurdles, but on the inside, our relationship with Christ is at a standstill!"

It is my conviction that service follows best on the heels of devotion. Service "goes better" after a quiet circle of time when God speaks to us and we speak to Him. Anyone knows a car cannot run on an empty tank.

We need to set aside a certain hour and place for time with our Lord. This daily meeting with God (whether it be in the early morning hours, at noon, or just before retiring) should be the focal point of our day. Just as God gives us strength for each new day, He gives us power for the day also.

The amount and kind of service we render is usually in proportion to the amount of time spent with God. Someone has said: "There are mysteries of grace and love on every page of the Bible; it is a thriving soul that finds the Book of God growing more and more precious."

One Thing Is Needful

Mary, the sister of Lazarus, learned this vital secret of receiving power from the Lord. The story of Mary and Martha has valuable lessons for us as Christian servants.

When Jesus visits in their home, we find Mary sitting at the feet of Jesus listening to His words. Where is Martha? We do not know, but probably she is busy in the kitchen, hurrying and scurrying around as many of us would be. I have always been able to identify with Martha. How like her I am.

Martha evidently is more domestically inclined than her sister, Mary. The Scripture says that Martha was "cumbered by much serving" (Luke 10:40).

Can't you hear her as she rushes a bit out of breath into the room where Jesus is tenderly talking with Mary about the things of God? "Lord, don't you think it's unfair that my sister just sits here while I do all the work?" "Tell her to come and help me."

The calm voice of Jesus covers the whole issue. "Martha, Martha, you are careful and troubled about many things, but one thing is needful, and Mary has chosen that good part, which shall not be taken away from her."

What had Mary chosen to do? She had chosen to sit at the feet of Jesus and learn from Him. Often, we must put aside what is seemingly important for the *most* important.

Mary is mentioned three times in the New Testament. Each time we find her at the feet of Jesus. This is about as close as you can get to a person. Mary loved Jesus and she demonstrated that love by pouring an expensive bottle of perfume upon His head and feet. It was a very extravagant thing to do and met with much disapproval, but Jesus said, "Let her alone; she has kept this for the day of my burial" (John 12:7).

Jesus does not condemn Mary for not taking care of her household duties. He is not saying that cleaning, cooking and serving are unimportant. He is saying that Martha is cumbered. She is troubled, hindered and burdened.

"Martha," Jesus is saying, "Why are you rushing around so? Mary has chosen that which is best, the one thing that is needful — the one thing that cannot be taken away from her."

What is that one thing? Jesus, Himself! Although it is not mentioned, I hope after Jesus' gentle words to Martha a change came about. I hope she was quick to see the work in which she had been so anxiously engaged was unimportant compared to Jesus' presence among them. I hope she put down her dishcloth and broom, or whatever she might have been holding, and that she, too, sat down at the Master's feet.

Martha Hands — Mary Heart

I must have the hands of Martha,
Hands that scrub and cook and sew —
I can have the heart of Mary
While I do these things, you know.

Though my hands are in the dishpan,
This soul of mine can soar
And in thoughts sublime and lofty
Go right up to heaven's door.

I must cook, oh endless dinners,
For my dear ones have to eat;
But my soul need not be cooking —
It can sit at Jesus' feet!

Help me, God while doing duties
Against which my soul rebels,
Be meekly still to peel potatoes,
But not grovel in the shells.

Grant me, God, mid things prosaic
Ere to choose the better part;
Grant that while I must be Martha
I may have the Mary heart.

— Author Unknown

Dear Loving Saviour, we want to live balanced lives in Your sight. Help us to make the right decisions between worship and service. Help us to intertwine them so much that one can scarcely tell when one has left off and the other has begun. In Jesus' name, Amen.

Mary has left us a good example. We need to plan our busy schedules with some moments to sit at the feet of Jesus. Mary Welch, in her delightful book *Reckoning at Dusk* has expressed this thought in a beautiful way:

> Martha learned to dedicate her many things. Like her, I must learn to season service with that luxury of love which can leave the dishes in the kitchen sink while I sit down for a quiet hour with the Master. Love must have feet to serve, and service must have knees that kneel.

Malnutrition of the Spirit

We need to study His Word intently and hungrily every day. Let us listen as God speaks to us through the Scriptures. Peter writes, "Like newborn babes, long for the pure milk of the Word that by it we may grow" (1 Peter 2:2). Do we *long* for the pure milk of His Word?

Jeremiah relates how important the Word of God should be:

> Your words were found, and I ate them,
> And Your word was to me the joy and rejoicing
> Of my heart: (Jeremiah 15:16).

Our appetites are trained so that we become hungry on a regular basis — three times a day. As a rule, we wouldn't think of missing a meal. In the same way, malnutrition of the spirit comes about swiftly when we do not hunger and thirst for His Word. Job said, "I have esteemed the words of His mouth more than my necessary food" (Job 23:12).

Remember, internal qualities effect external servanthood!

Kept for Him

My mind was so full of service
   I had drifted from Him apart,
And He longed for the old confiding,
   The union of heart with heart.
I sought and received forgiveness,
   While my eyes with tears were dim,
And now though the work is still precious,
   The first place is kept for Him!

— Author Unknown

To Serve Him Forever

In the 21st chapter of Exodus, we find these words:

> If you buy a Hebrew servant, he shall serve six years; and in the seventh he shall go out free and pay nothing.
>
> If he comes in by himself, he shall go out by himself; if he comes in married, then his wife shall go out with him.
>
> If his master has given him a wife, and she has borne him sons or daughters, the wife and her children shall be her master's, and he shall go out by himself.
>
> But if the servant plainly says, "I love my master, my wife, and my children; I will not go out free,"
>
> Then his master shall bring him to the judges. He shall also bring him to the door, or to the doorpost, and his master shall pierce his ear with an awl; and he shall serve him forever (Exodus 21:2-6).

An *awl* was a sharp pointed instrument which was used to pierce the ear of a servant who chose to serve his master and stay with him forever.

There must have been a great hole after his ear was punctured. We have no idea whether he wore an earring or not. Whatever the case, the pierced ear symbolized that this man was a perpetual slave.

In Psalm 40:6 we read: "Sacrifice and offering you did not desire; My ears you have opened;" Literally translated the last part of this verse should be: "My ears you have digged (or pierced) through."

David, the writer of this hymn is saying, "I am your servant and will serve you always." In the 8th verse he goes on to say, "I delight to do Your will, O my God." This is most certainly an illusion to the custom of piercing the ear of the servant who refused to go free.

Should we make the decision to be perpetual slaves to Christ, we will honor Him by "delighting to do His will." We will refuse to follow the attractions of this world which only offer superficial "freedom." When we follow Him, we are "free indeed" (John 8:36).

We may or may not have pierced ears. Whether we do or not, let us allow our Lord to pierce our ears spiritually. Let us say to our Father in heaven:

> I want to be Your perpetual slave and servant. I will remain with You forever. I will never leave You, just as I rest in Your promise to never leave me.

Timothy wrote a loving message of concern to slaves who were under bondage to their masters, but the message certainly applies to us as well:

> **Let as many servants as are under the yoke count their own masters worthy of honor, so that the name of God and His doctrine may not be blasphemed (1 Timothy 6:1).**

We as Christian servants are under bondage no longer because of "the liberty by which Christ has made us free" (Galatians 5:1). We have One Master and He is indeed worthy of honor.

Pierce My Ear

Pierce my ear, Oh Lord my God,
Take me to Your door this day.
I will serve no other God,
Lord, I'm here to stay.

For You have paid the price for me
With Your blood you set me free.
I will serve You eternally —
A free man I'll never be.

— Author Unknown

Personal Security

What is personal security? It is knowing *who* we are, and to *Whom* we belong. We have perfect assurance of Who controls our service. We know the reason and purpose of our existence.

> ... for I know whom I have believed and am persuaded that He is able to keep what I have committed to Him until that day (2 Timothy 1:12).

A personal security in Christ helps us relax. It helps us trust Him for every thing we need when we go out to serve. Through Scripture and perfect confidence in Him, we are "thoroughly equipped for every good work" (2 Timothy 3:17).

We look to Him for motivation, strength and ability. Trusting Him, we serve gratefully and with joy, never doubting His presence. My favorite verse for others and myself is Proverbs 3:5 and 6:

> Trust in the Lord with all your heart,
> And lean not on your own understanding;
> In all your ways acknowledge Him,
> And He shall direct your paths.

In seeking to serve, we are to acknowledge Him first and foremost. He will direct our steps in paths of service.

Secure in Christ

To be secure in Christ frees us from the blinding fear that our service might be misunderstood or misdirected. For sure, we are all going to make mistakes when we reach out to others. Mistakes sometimes occur that we might learn from them. Not everyone is going to appreciate and welcome our help. Failure to please should never keep us from serving another.

None of us can please everyone all the time. The sooner we learn this, the more relaxed we will be. We possess a valuable and powerful knowledge . . . "Christ in me, the hope of Glory!" (Colossians 1:27). Wisdom and knowledge about people come with experience and age.

God expects us to show mercy, understanding and kindness — not to react to every childish snub. Maturity in Christ brings deeper, wider, firmer security. The peace of God which transcends knowledge is the beautiful result.

Personal security in Christ brings confidence in self. We are able to say: "Hey, we are important to Christ, therefore we must be important to the person we are attempting to help." We may *feel* inadequate, but with Christ we can say, "I can do all things through Christ who strengthens me" (Philippians 4:13).

The Lord Loves Through Us

Have you ever considered that there is nothing good we can do apart from the help of the Lord? Where do we think our love and caring spirit comes from? It comes from the Lord who loves through us. None of us will ever obtain the servant's spirit without God's indwelling Spirit.

Service comes naturally and freely from a heart which trusts completely in Him. Filled with faith and confidence, we can do unbelievable things in His name and for His glory.

Sometimes we sit on the banks of a pond or lake and suddenly we see ripples on the water. Where did they originate? No one knows, but it is exciting to think that those ripples were made by someone. Wouldn't it be wonderful if our lives were one continual ripple?

The astonishing discovery that we are not alone and never shall be, places our service in new dimensions. A new perspective replaces the old idea that we have to be beautiful, talented and brilliant people to do much good in this world. The most ordinary people (and there are no ordinary people in the kingdom) can do great and wonderful things for Him.

God Be With You

May His Counsels Sweet uphold you,
And His Loving Arms enfold you,
As you journey on your way.

May His Sheltering Wings protect you,
And His Light Divine direct you,
Turning darkness into day.

May His Potent Peace surround you,
And His Presence linger with you,
As your inner, golden ray.

— Author Unknown

CHAPTER SEVEN

SOMETHING TO THINK ABOUT TODAY

1. Relate to one other person today the illustration about the upper and lower basin. Does this make any difference about how you feel about service?
2. What were the two secrets of the worthy woman's service?
3. Where did she obtain her strength? Where do we obtain our strength?
4. How can we find the necessary strength to continue pouring out loving service?
5. How can we help Him carry out His plans in the world?
6. We do not give enough attention to the importance of the _____ in devotion and service.
7. Satan comes as an _____ ___ _____, working on our _____.
8. True or False?
   A. We need not worry about over extending ourselves.
   B. Activity and service are synonymous.
   C. It's possible for us to participate in every service we are asked to do.
   D. A mature Christian is one who has learned to balance activities and service on one hand, and the stewardship of mental, physical and emotional health on the other.
9. Why is a daily meeting with God so vital?
10. The amount and kind of service we undertake is usually in proportion to _____ _____ ___ _____ _____ _____ _____.
11. Why did Jesus tell Mary that she had chosen the better part?
12. How can each one of us suffer spiritual malnutrition?
13. What is personal security? Why is it important?
14. Turn to Colossians 1:27, and give the triumphant formula for personal security.
15. Whenever we are feeling inadequate, what one verse fortifies us the most?
16. Discuss this statement: "A new perspective replaces the old idea that we have to be beautiful, talented and brilliant people to do much good in this world."

CHAPTER 8

A HUMBLE SPIRIT

What does it mean to be humble? William Temple stated it this way:

> Humility does not mean thinking less of yourself than of other people, nor does it mean having a low opinion of your own gifts. It means freedom from thinking about yourself one way or the other at all.

How Peter Learned Humility

Impulsive, impetuous Peter learned the grace of humility by following, learning from, and observing the speech and attitude of His Master. He learned it to such a degree, that he was able to write in his first epistle:

> Yes, all of you be submissive to one another, and be clothed with humility, for God resists the proud, but gives grace to the humble (1 Peter 5:5).

> Therefore humble yourselves under the mighty hand of God, that He may exalt you in due time (1 Peter 5:6).

James wrote much the same thing in his book:

> Humble yourselves in the sight of the Lord, and He will lift you up (James 4:10).

Certainly the Christian woman who desires to cultivate the servant's spirit will place humility at the top of the list. Becoming humble is not easy in this day and time, when "looking after number one" is the goal of many. It is easy for any of us to feel superior to another person.

Tozier wrote:

> I have met two classes of Christians: The proud who imagine they are humble, and the humble who are afraid they are proud. There should be a third class: The self-forgetful who leave the whole thing in the hands of Christ and refuse to waste any time trying to make themselves good and humble. They will reach the goal far ahead of the rest of us.

Lowliness

Paul advised:

> Let nothing be done through selfish ambition and conceit, but in lowliness of mind let each esteem others better than himself. Let each of you look not only for his own interests, but also for the interests of others (Phillipians 2:3,4).

How is it possible for Christian women to put aside the ideology of the present age and to exhibit humility in serving others? What does it mean to have "lowliness of mind?" It is the opposite of being proud. The Greek word for humble is *tapeinos* which means "low-lying." It is interesting that humility and lowliness are both associated with the mind.

Paul's Humility

When Paul was in Miletus, waiting to go to Jerusalem, he sent for the elders of the church in Ephesus. When they had arrived and were gathered to hear what he had to say, he told them:

> You know from the first day that I came to Asia, in what manner I always lived among you, serving the Lord with all humility, with many tears and trials which happened to me by the plotting of the Jews; (Acts 20-18,19).

In this writing, we learn that humility here is rendered "humility of mind." Paul's mind had become humble from "looking unto Jesus." In the same manner, our minds will become humble as we fix our eyes upon Him. When Paul wrote his great treatise on love, he mentioned one of the most significant aspects of love:

> Love suffers long and is kind; love does not envy; love does not parade itself, is not puffed up (1 Corinthians 13:4).

John Gibson recognized this factor when he wrote the following:

You Can't Strut Before God

> Have you ever seen anyone who was so proud that "He could strut sitting down?" How easy it is to lull ourselves into thinking that we are smarter, better or more loved by God than anyone else.
>
> Maybe it would be well for all men to remember that God "made *from one* every nation of men to live on the face of the earth." We all "live and move and have our being" in Him.
>
> Nor should we count too much on our scholastic attainments as evidence that somehow we have broken away from the ordinary clay of mankind. If we are tempted to be puffed up by our knowledge rather than humbled by our ignorance we might do well to consider a recent newspaper want-ad: "Job opening for one who has an M.A. and a Ph.D, or two weeks of practical experience."
>
> We may strut like peacocks before one another, but God goes on choosing the foolish, the weak, the low and despised, "even things that are not, to bring to nothing things that are." The high and the mighty are shamed. "There is no place for human pride in the presence of God."

Paul continually emphasized the importance of humility. In writing to the church in Rome, he admonished:

> Be of the same mind toward one another. Do not set your mind on high things, but associate with the humble. Do not be wise in your own opinion (Romans 12:16).

Our Greatest Example

Our greatest example of humility was demonstrated by our Lord in the 13th chapter of John.

At supper with His twelve disciples, Jesus arose and took off His robe. At the same time He girded himself with a towel. This shocked His disciples to the core. They could not imagine why their Master would degrade Himself to the degree of adorning the clothing of a slave. A towel wrapped around the body symbolized a lowly servant.

He was willing to take the servant's place. Humility was His natural role — He could be nothing less than Himself. He said in Luke 22:27: "I am among you as the One who serves." Jesus simply and humbly wanted to serve His apostle friends as well as teach them a lesson they were never to forget.

> After that, He poured water into a basin and began to wash the disciple's feet, and to wipe them with the towel with which He was girded (John 13:5).

Jesus had seen what they were too blind to see. A servant was not present to wash their dirty feet! In those days everyone wore sandals. It was the custom for the master of the house to provide a basin of water and a servant to wash the feet of the guests.

The apostles were not about to do this undignified act, even if they had noticed the need. "Let one of the others do it," they might have been thinking. "I'm certainly not going to stoop so low."

After washing all the disciple's feet, including Peter's, after quite a hassle, Jesus put his robe on again and sat down. "Do you know what I have done to you?" He asked. None of them answered. How could they? Not one of them understood and, if they had made a polite guess, they were still too shocked to answer.

Jesus had shown them He was Lord and Teacher. Now He wanted them to know what it really meant to be a servant. Jesus knew what was in man. He knew their thoughts and motives. He knew that unless He demonstrated real servanthood, they would never grasp the concept of greatness in God's Kingdom.

Let us make it our "forever" goal simply to be a servant as was Jesus. When we are humbly serving others, we are most like Christ. He came to demonstrate how to serve. True servanthood comes about only when we are willing to take off our robe of dignity and adorn ourselves with the towel of a slave.

Someone has said: "Too many people are seeking a pedestal and a throne, rather than a towel and basin." If we can only learn to humble ourselves in the sight of God, He will in due time, lift us up.

Jesus said:

> You call me Teacher and Lord, and you say well, for so I am. If I then, your Lord and Teacher, have washed your feet, you also ought to wash one another's feet. For I have given you an example, that you should do as I have done to you (John 13:13-15).

Lynn Anderson said: "When Christ washed His disciple's feet, we saw God on His knees doing slave labor."

Now, let us make five observations:

When we begin washing the feet of our fellow disciples it may mean:

1. Opening ourselves up to criticism and misunderstanding.
2. Risking the disapproval of others.
3. Losing dignity and pride.
4. Disregarding the pious opinions of those who wouldn't be caught dead in the garb of a servant.
5. Serving voluntarily instead of being asked.
6. Getting involved with dirt, disorder, uncleanliness, filth and foul smells. (Dirty feet aren't all that appealing you know).

No experience is learned until it is practiced. How can we know the happiness Jesus described in the following verses, unless we try it out for ourselves? Head knowledge can never take the place of actual experience.

> Most assuredly, I say to you, a servant is not greater than his master; nor is he who is sent

greater than he who sent him. If you know these things, happy are you if you do them (John 13:16,17).

"Happy are you if you *do* them." The funny thing about this is that all the time we think we are humbling ourselves before others, we are actually blessing ourselves!

Imitation of Christ

Do you remember the way Paul described service in Ephesians 6:6 and 7?

> . . . not with eyeservice, as men-pleasers, but as servants of Christ, doing the will of God from the heart, with good will doing service, as to the Lord, and not to men.

When His disciples were disputing among themselves over who would be the greatest, Jesus lovingly pointed out to them:

> Yet it shall not be among you; but whoever desires to become great among you shall be your servant. And whoever of you desires to be first shall be slave of all. For even the Son of Man did not come to be served, but to serve, and to give His life a ransom for many (Mark 10:43-45).

Let us imitate the servant heart of Jesus, giving ourselves in humble service to make this world a better place in which to live.

The Fable Of The Trees

The fable of the trees as found in Judges 9:8-15 is probably the best known fable in the Bible. It teaches a valuable lesson in humility:

> The trees once went forth
> to anoint a king over them,
> And they said to the olive tree,
> "Reign over us!"

But the olive tree said to them,
"Should I cease giving my oil,
With which they honor God and men,
And go to sway over trees?"

Then the trees said to the fig tree,
"You come and reign over us!"
But the fig tree said to them,
"Should I cease my sweetness
and my good fruit,
And go to sway over trees?"

Then the trees said to the vine,
"You come and reign over us!"
But the vine said to them,
"Should I cease my new wine,
Which cheers both God and men,
And go to sway over trees?"

Then all the trees said to the bramble,
"You come and reign over us!"
And the bramble said to the trees,
"If in truth you anoint me as king over you,
Then come and take shelter in my shade;
But if not, let fire come out of the bramble
And devour the cedars of Lebanon!"

   The first three trees had been invited by the other trees to be king over the forest. Though flattered, and probably very enticed, they could not forget the important place they already were filling.
   The olive tree remembered that the oil pressed from its fruit is used for offerings, medicine, food and light. The olive tree was not willing to give up its purpose — that of honoring God and mankind.
   The fig tree also served a great purpose. It produces a fruit which is sweet and delicious, a happy combination which brings joy to many who partake of its sweetness.
   The grape vine knew its value and could not be tempted. The fruit of the vine is a source of cheer and comfort.
   All of these trees knew their value. They chose service instead of fame and renown. They chose wisely and well. The greatest servants never seek to rule over others or to be known in a great

way. They simply give their best and find their reward in the good they do and the pleasure they bring.

When the bramble bush was asked to be king he was flattered and became haughty. Though worthless and idle, he became puffed up and arrogant. "Come and take shelter in *my* shade," he said. Pride and boastfulness had become part of his demeanor.

Gideon's Humble Attitude

In contrast to the bramble bush, Gideon was a man with a humble attitude. He was like the first three trees mentioned in the fable.

> Then the men of Israel said to Gideon, "Rule over us, both you and your son, and your grandson also; for you have delivered us from the hand of Midian." But Gideon said to them, "I will not rule over you, nor shall my son rule over you; the Lord shall rule over you" (Judges 8:22,23).

Gideon was beloved in God's sight because of His humility and lack of pride. God lifts up the humble and rewards those who simply want to serve Him.

The Humble, Unrecognized Jobs

In order for any of us to be pleasing to God, somewhere along the path of servanthood, we must rid ourselves of pride and humble ourselves in the sight of the Lord.

This may mean taking on some lowly, unrecognized jobs, such as serving in the nursery or cleaning up after a church fellowship.

When we come to the glorious recognition of all our Lord has done for us, we will not mind the humble tasks that we are called to perform.

I like the statement someone has made: "God did not call us to be a sensation He called us to be servants." The sooner we believe and act upon this premise, the happier our lives will be.

My Turn in the Nursery

Last Sunday was my turn in the nursery to work.
My heart wasn't in it; my feelings were hurt.
A child from its mother did not want to part
And it cried a lot with its broken heart.

I prayed that soon the hour would end
Then I could relax — no more children to tend.
Soon the hour was over; it felt so good to be free
I said, "Once a month is too much for me!"

That very Sunday as I sat in the pew
A very good sermon, but visitors were few.
But down came a woman and her soul was saved.
She was the mother of that crying babe!

Then it dawned on me that I had been a part
Of her being saved — of giving God her heart.
From that day on I would never dread
Working in the nursery while souls are fed.

— Author Unknown

Sound No Trumpet

We are reminded of our dear Lord's words in Matthew 6:2:

> Therefore when you do a charitable deed, do not sound a trumpet before you as the hypocrites do in the synagogues and in the streets, that they may have glory from men. Assuredly, I say to you, they have their reward.

We are never to sound a trumpet before us as we serve people. We are to humbly and reverently serve God with a heart of compassion, kindness and love toward our fellow man. When a "trumpet is sounded," it robs God of the glory. He deserves the praise for all good works. The sound of the trumpet should never be heard among God's humble servants.

Sound of the Trumpet

Sound no trumpet
Sing no song of praise
Unto yourself.
Blare no horn of triumph
As you walk.
Crash no cymbals before you.
Remember
That you are but a speck
In a star-filled sky.
One tiny drop alone
In a sea of tears.
But strip your soul of pride
And bow your head and weep.
For all that you may ever do
Is but a moment in Eternity.
Do not swagger when you walk,
But crawl upon your knees.
Clothe your soul with lowliness
Follow your Star with faith.
Except for His great love
Your soul would die.
Sound no trumpet for yourself,
But praise His Holy Name.
Give Him the glory of your life,
And He will give His peace.

— Author Unknown

CHAPTER EIGHT

SOMETHING TO THINK ABOUT TODAY

1. "Therefore _____ yourselves under the mighty hand of God, that He may _____ you in due time" (1 Peter 5,6).
2. List three requirements for humility found in Philippians 2:3 and 4:
   1.
   2.
   3.
3. What does it mean to have "lowliness of mind?"
4. Our greatest example of humility was demonstrated by _____ when He _____ _____ _____ _____.
5. When are we most like Christ?
6. Discuss the statement "Too many people are seeking a pedestal and a throne, rather than a towel and basin."
7. Why did Jesus wash His apostle's feet?
8. Discuss the six risks we take in "washing" the feet of our fellow disciples.
9. No experience is learned until it is _____.
10. What lessons do we learn from the Fable of the Trees?
11. Why was Gideon so beloved in God's sight?
12. God did not call us to be a _____, He called us to be _____.
13. What does it mean to "sound a trumpet before us?"
14. When a trumpet is sounded, it robs _____ of _____.

CHAPTER NINE

A WINSOME SPIRIT

Kalos

There are two Greek words defined as "good." The first is the Greek word *agathos* which means "a quality of goodness." The second is derived from the Greek word *kalos*. It is a word that is used more than one hundred times in the New Testament.

Kalos describes someone or something that not only has a quality of goodness, but goes beyond. *Kalos* is a description of that person or object which is attractive, lovely and winsome. I like that word — winsome!

Every Christian should have a winsome personality — one that glows inside out with the beauty of Jesus. Just as a prism picks up the facets of the sunshine and reflects them in many colors and shapes on nearby surfaces, so the woman in love with the Lord radiates the many facets of His love.

Our service should not only be helpful, it should be pleasing and beautiful as well. Winsomeness attracts and blesses as much as it serves.

A Joyful, Free Spirit

A winsome spirit is a lovely thing to behold. It bubbles over (like a fountain) from a joyful, free spirit, and brings that quality of joy and rejoicing to everyone around. It is wholesome, appealing and magnetic. In 2 Corinthians 5:20 we discover that God makes His appeal through us! Are we appealing? Winsomeness is not cloaked in deceit or false pride. It cannot be faked. It is relaxed and serene . . . fun to observe and fun to be around. It imparts strength, yet rests one with its sheer charm. It is graceful and truly beautiful. A man or woman endowed with godly winsomeness is a fascinating servant of God. In demeanor and conduct, they manifest the "beauty of holiness."

Good Works

> Let your light so shine before men, that they may see your good works and glorify your Father in heaven (Matthew 5:16).

Throughout the Scriptures the words "good works" or "good deeds" are translated as *kalos* — winsome acts of service. Hebrews 10:24 illustrates this by saying, "And let us consider one another in order to stir up love and good works."

In Titus 2:7 we find that we are to be a pattern (example) of good works. In verse 14, we discover as God's special people we are to be zealous (which means burning or on fire) of good works.

God's glorious light should be reflected in every area of our lives — especially in Christian service. If we allow the Lord to keep on transforming us, our service to others will be winsome and lovely to behold.

Service which is performed dutifully and perfunctoriusly is fine, but how much more appealing is the sight of a Christian man or woman serving with winsome joy, humor and cheer.

The attractive (kalos) loveliness and beauty seen in the life and manner of Christians is the essence which draws others to know and love the Lord. *Kalos* is the sweetest word to describe Christian service.

Madeline L'Engle says:

> We do not draw people to Christ by loudly discrediting what they believe, by telling them how wrong they are and how right we are, but by showing them a light that is so lovely they will want with all their hearts to know the source of it.

After we have shown others the light, we need to carefully teach them. How will they know how to obey the Lord unless we point the way?

> A woman's love is like a light
> Shining the brightest in the night
> And a woman's love we hardly know
> Until we need a hand to help
> A light to lead —
> Then woman's love
> Is light indeed.
> — Author Unknown

Gentleness — A Part of Winsomeness

1 Peter 3:3-6 has always been a guiding force in my life:

> Your beauty should not come from outward adornment, such as braided hair and the wearing of gold jewelry and fine clothes. Instead it should be that of your inner self, the unfading beauty of a gentle and quiet spirit, which is of great worth in God's sight. For this is the way the holy women of the past who put their hope in God used to make themselves beautiful. (NIV)

To think that gentle-spirited people are precious in God's eyes! Winsome people are gentle hearted people. It is a natural inclination for those who love the Lord and want to imitate Him. Gentleness is a trait borne by the Spirit, for it is one of His fruit (Galatians 5:22).

Gentleness is a sweet and gracious garment that a Christian woman may wear at all times; not just for special occasions. Gentle-hearted persons have a gift in warming, soothing, hushing and quieting dispirited little people, as well as resting and calming weary-worn husbands. The Greek word for gentleness is *epiekes*, translated "sweet reasonableness." I like that term. If we can cultivate this trait, then our lives will bless others — tempering every adversity.

In 2 Timothy 2:24 we read: "And a servant of the Lord must not quarrel, but be gentle to all, able to teach, patient..."

One cannot have a griping, complaining, boastful, harsh attitude and still be the Lord's servant. A brisk, "no-nonsense" approach to servanthood will turn people away. We must be "winsome" to win some! A lack of gentleness denotes a lack of love and caring. People who are so treated will feel like objects instead of human beings with real needs. We need to demonstrate patience while listening to our friends as they tell us where it hurts. Everyone needs someone who will listen gently without condemning.

In this winsome and sweet invitation we find comfort and consolation:

> Come to Me, all you who labor and are heavy laden, and I will give you rest. Take my yoke upon you and learn from Me, for I am gentle and lowly in heart, and you will find rest for your souls. For

my yoke is easy and My burden is light (Matthew 11:28-30).

Jesus said that He was gentle and lowly — at the same time asking us to "learn from Him." He was so gentle that it was impossible for Him to break a reed or extinguish a candle. He walked the streets of Galilee and lived among men "yet never raised His voice in the streets." He was the lowliest and most humble-gentle person that ever lived.

Throughout his wonderful writings to the Corinthians, Paul indicated that he was meek when he was among them, but bold when he was absent from them. His letters were fervent in Spirit as he pleaded with them "by the meekness and gentleness of Christ." This Christ-like spirit had rubbed off on Paul to the extent that he could demonstrate the "quiet gentle spirit' too. He had learned it in the school room of Christ.

> He will feed His flock like a shepherd;
> He will gather the lambs
> with His arm,
> And carry them in His bosom,
> And gently lead those who are
> Young (Isaiah 40:11).

Teachers of Good Things

Older women (and we are all older than someone) are to be "teachers of good things" (Titus 2:3). It is so sweet to see an older woman help a younger woman with a soft, tender touch. Young wives and mothers have much to bear. Sometimes their burdens are almost too much to bear.

A mature woman who has had experiences through many years of living and learning, can be a "balm of Gilead" to a tired, weary-worn little mom or wife. Her gentle words and warm embraces can soothe and comfort perhaps like no one else. She is like a river ever flowing toward the shoreline, ever giving of herself.

In my daily devotional book, *New Day Dawning,* I wrote:

> I have been sitting under a big oak tree on a bench beside the lake. I have had a wonderful prayer and Bible reading time. As I sit and gaze at the lake, I ponder my book *Ripples on the Water.* The calm, placid lake shines this morn-

ing with the soft, easy-going waves rippling in one direction — toward the shore line.

Serenity and peace fill my spirit as I "drink in" the gentleness which calms my heart. The servant's spirit should be like this too, I think. Gentle and easy, asking nothing but to give to the shore line and impart tranquillity in doing so.

Someone has written this beautiful description of a gentle spirit:

> To live gently is to live on tiptoe in the presence of God all day. It is to embrace the unfolding dawn and to kiss the dewdrops upon the forehead of day. It is to pour oneself out like flakes of snow upon the winter scars of strife in other lives. Gentle looks and love's fingers upon fevered brows and gentle words are love's kisses upon parched lips.

Philippians 4:5 says, "Let your gentleness be known to all men. The Lord is at hand." Phillips translation puts it this way: "Have a reputation for gentleness, and never forget the nearness of your Lord."

How can we learn to be gentle and kind? The Holy Spirit is our teacher. Gentleness stems from "keeping in step with the Spirit" (Galatians 5:25).

Because the Lord is "always at hand" we want to be pleasing and acceptable in His sight. He is our model of gentleness — He will show us how. In search of greater wisdom in cultivating the servant's heart, we must remember all spiritual wisdom comes from above.

> But the wisdom that is from above is first pure, then peaceable, gentle, willing to yield, full of mercy and good fruits, without partiality, and without hypocrisy. Now the fruit of righteousness is sown in peace by those who make peace (James 3:17,18).

Our actions continually are making ripples on the water of life. Are they peaceful, calm ripples of love radiating in all directions? Or, are they waves of destruction and calamity?

Kindness Is a Part of Winsomeness

"Love suffers long and is kind" (1 Corinthians 13:4). Kindness is a character trait greatly needed by every servant of God. Without kindness, little understanding or mercy would be shown to others. The word kindness comes from the Greek word *chrestos* which means serviceable, good, pleasant, gracious, and I might add *generous*. A kind person is sweet and generous in words and action. Gentleness is translated kindness in the New Kings James Bible. Gentle kindness is "sweet graciousness" in my estimation.

It is said of the excellent woman in Proverbs 31:26: "She opens her mouth with wisdom, and on her tongue is the law of kindness."

What does "the law of kindness" mean? Kind words and actions are the habit of her life. She practices kindness daily without forethought. It is a part of her demeanor, because *her heart is kind*. Unless the heart of a person is kind, no amount of pretending will suffice. Shakespeare wrote: "Kindness in a woman, not her beauteous looks, shall win my love."

When a woman is rich in kindness she is rich in all. She doesn't need fame, fortune or beauty to make her life a lovely overflow.

If You Were Busy

If you were busy being kind,
Before you knew it you would find
You'd soon forget to think tis true
That someone else was unkind to you.

If you were busy being glad,
And cheering people who are sad,
Although your heart might ache a bit,
You'd soon forget to notice it.

If you were busy being good,
And doing just the best you could,
You'd not have time to blame some man
Who's doing just the best he can.

If you were busy being true
To what you know you ought to do,
You'd be so busy you'd forget
The blunders of the folks you've met.

> If you were busy being right,
> You'd find yourself too busy, quite,
> To criticize your neighbor long
> Because he's being wrong.
>
> — Author Unknown

Someone has said: "You cannot do a kindness too soon because you never know how soon it will be too late."

Spontaneity Is a Part of Winsomeness

We have learned that heart-felt gentleness and kindness are requirements in genuine service. Spontaneity is another quality of the Christian servant. Acting immediately upon our good impulses is often better than delaying action "until we feel like it" or waiting until the spirit moves us.

Often we put off until tomorrow doing things that should be performed today. We simply do not listen to our hearts. The impulses which prompt us to call a troubled person, visit a grieved one or write a note to someone are seldom wrong.

There will certainly be times when we are rebuffed, but for the most part a kind word or deed performed spontaneously from the heart may make the difference between despair and hopefulness.

Many of us plan our time and organize our days without a thought to the minutes and hours which should be spent in spontaneous service. We fill our calendars and schedules with appointments, block out periods of time for work and entertainment, but how many of us leave free time for those persons who will be coming in and out of our lives? What about individuals who turn to us for help or encouragement? Are they going to be turned aside or ignored because they do not fit into our schedules?

Some of life's most fulfilling moments are experienced when opportunities are seized and acted upon. Surprised by interruptions? Pause to praise a God who has enough confidence in us to send someone to serve. Paul said in 1 Corinthians 9:19:

> For though I am free from all men, I have made
> myself a servant to all, that I might win the more.

Ways of Being Winsome

1. Smile

> "A smile is a light in the window that shows someone is at home."

The dictionary has this to say about the word "smile." "To have or take on a facial expression showing pleasure, amusement, affection, friendliness, irony, derision, etc; and characterized by an upward curving of the corners of the mouth and a sparkling of the eye."

To me that is the best part of a smile . . . the sparkle in the eye. I have a friend that I have never seen without a smile. Oh, I have seen a tear or two, especially when she lost her twin sister, but the lovely expression on her face, the twinkle in her eye, makes her captivating.

We've all heard the expression, "Smile! God loves you!" What better reason to smile than to know we are accepted and loved? No one has better reason to smile and be happy than the Christian servant. God has done so much for all of us.

I like the tongue in cheek expression: "Smile! It makes people wonder what you are up to!" A smile indicates a deep down joy which cannot be contained. It bubbles up over the top and splashes on everyone.

> A merry heart does good like a medicine but a broken spirit dries the bones (Proverbs 17:22).

I have heard it said that "A smile is not just a wide mouth when it gets its start in love. It starts in the soul and ripples outward, touching everything."

> They might not need me,
>   but they might.
> I'll let my head be just in sight.
> A smile as small as mine might be
>   precisely their necessity.
>
> — Emily Dickinson

2. Cheerfulness

We all like to be around cheerful people, don't we? Do others like to be around us? Are we fun? Do we make people feel better just by being near us? Do we cheer people so that when they go away they feel more able to cope?

A cheerful spirit should be the mark of anyone who seeks to develop the servant's spirit. A cheerful expression is the most beautiful cosmetic you'll ever wear. A smile encourages others to come out of the darkness into the sunlight of God's redemptive love.

Thoughtful Words

How many words have you spoken this day
Designed to encourage and cheer?
How oft, may I ask, went you out of your way
To gladden the hearts of those near?
You may lift a burden and lighten a load
Make sadness and gloom disappear,
By being more thoughtful of others nearby
Through a word that is warm and sincere.

— D.W. Dryden Sinclair

Joseph Addison wrote that "Cheerfulness is the best promoter of health, and is as friendly to the mind as to the body." One of the most precious gifts we can give to others is the gift of cheer and happiness. Abraham Lincoln said, "You are about as happy as you make up your mind to be."

I read about a girl who had been born with a physical handicap. She carried her affliction with her all life long. Yet, whenever she spoke, she bubbled over with joy and cheer. Someone finally asked her why she had such a happy spirit.

> "When I was a little girl," she replied, "my mother told me that perhaps I might never be able to do many things that others could do. She told me that it was up to me to choose my attitude. I could be miserable and make others feel that way, too, or I could choose to be happy and cheerful. I decided then that my ministry would be that of spreading cheer and gladness to everyone who came into my sphere of influence. Spreading cheer makes me feel that way too."

Someone has written:

> To spread cheer wherever we go, to find contentment in small pleasures, to be ever thankful, to practice kindness instead of harshness — this is the ministry of the Christian woman.

The writer of Proverbs has said: "A joyful heart makes a cheerful face, but when the heart is sad, the spirit is broken" (Proverbs 15:13). This verse proves that joy is an "inside job," doesn't it?

The Ideal Woman

What is your conception of the ideal woman? I thought about this, and decided:

> My ideal woman is one who has a winsomeness in her personality; a twinkle in her eye; a smile on her face; a lilt in her voice; a spring in her step; a charm in her demeanor; a song on her lips; a kindness on her tongue, a glow on her cheeks; a wholesomeness in her mind; a sweetness in her expression; a neatness in her appearance; a gentleness in her spirit, a hope in her soul and a love in her heart.
>
> A woman like this brings color, joy and serenity to everyone she meets. She is beautiful even without cosmetics . . . is lovely without a perfect figure. A woman like this brings us closer to the reality of purity and holiness. She helps us see that in these days of sin and ugliness, there is still someone who emulates the image of Jesus Christ.
>
> A wife and mother need not be glamorous and exotic to be a queen. When she has these traits, her husband and children will "rise up and call her blessed." What more could a woman desire?

Lovely Winsomeness

Henry Drummond said: "The greatest thing a man can do for his heavenly Father is to be kind to His other children."

We are not in this world to gather happiness — we are here to give it away. There should be a deep love and compassion in our winsomeness. Each of us should draw from the well of God's great love, drink . . . then pass the dipper to others. The gracious, winsome heart draws others to *Him,* who was and is the most winsome Servant of all.

> The New Testament holds that the best missionary method which the church possesses is the truly Christian life. It holds that men are to be attracted, far more than argued into the Christian life. There should be in the life of the Christian not only goodness, but also a loveliness, which will make all men and women desire the secret which is His.
>
> — Author Unknown

I would like to warm the hearts of women everywhere with a gentle reminder that there is nothing sweeter in this world than being God's woman. When we are living in the will of our gracious and loving Father, there is absolutely nothing more to be desired. Life is the most precious when faith is cherished and nurtured. Those who live in daily contact with us cannot help but feel the deeper glow. God needs warm, loving, tender hearts to take care of His little ones.

CHAPTER NINE

SOMETHING TO THINK ABOUT TODAY

1. What two Greek words can be used for the word "good?"
2. What does *Kalos* mean?
3. How would you describe a winsome person?
4. In 2 Corinthians 5:20 we discover God makes His _____ _____ _____.
5. Winsomeness is not cloaked in _____ or _____ _____.
6. A winsome spirit is also a _____ spirit.
7. How is the grace of god expressed most fully in the New Testament?
8. What quality draws others to know and love the Lord?
9. _____ _____ people are precious in God's eyes.
10. A lack of gentleness denotes a lack of _____ and _____.
11. Jesus was so gentle, it was impossible for Him _____ _____, or _____ a _____.
12. Older women are to be _____ _____ _____.
13. Philippians 4:5 says "Let your _____ to all men."
14. How can we learn to be gentle and kind?
15. Describe spiritual wisdom as defined in James 3:17 and 18.
16. The excellent woman in Proverbs 31:26 opened her mouth with wisdom and on her tongue was the law of kindness. What does this mean?
17. Name two ways we can be winsome.
18. What is the most beautiful cosmetic we'll ever wear?
19. We are not here in this world to gather _____, we are here to _____ _____ _____.
20. There is nothing sweeter in the world than being _____ _____.

CHAPTER 10

A NEIGHBORLY SPIRIT

Who Is My Neighbor?

The dictionary defines a neighbor as "someone who lives near another." However, you and I know from the teaching of the Good Samaritan and other passages of Scripture that a neighbor is anyone who needs our help.

When the sarcastic lawyer tested Jesus by asking Him, "And who is my neighbor?" Jesus replied by relating the parable of the Good Samaritan. Then He turned to the lawyer, surprising Him with this question: "So which of these three do you think was neighbor to him who fell among the thieves?"

After the lawyer thought about it awhile he answered, "He who showed mercy on him." Then Jesus said to him, "Go and do likewise" Luke 10:37).

Jesus is calling us today to "go and do likewise." We are to live among our neighbors as helpers, servants and friends. The question is not, "Who is my neighbor?" but "What kind of neighbor am I?"

Service in the Neighborhood

One of the best places a woman can serve is right in her own neighborhood. I believe our neighborhoods, in many cases, are extensions of our homes.

My neighborhood is made up of various families all manifesting a diversity of interests, cultures and needs. There are husbands and wives with marital problems, troubled teenagers, lonely widows and discontented housewives.

In every neighborhood, yours as well as mine, we will find people who are hurting, who are sad and mixed-up. In order for any of us to obey God's command to "go and do likewise" we are in great need of a merciful spirit. Neighborly acts of mercy such as a kind word, a tender soft embrace, and a warm smile are greatly needed in a world which has lost its direction and purpose.

Our Small World

Is my neighborhood a better place because I live in it? Do my next door neighbors know that I am a Christian? Do Evelyn and Gaty know about my values and my faith in Christ? Do they know that Christ is the center of my life, and everything else is the circumference? Do they know by the behavior of my children that I am training them up in the nurture of the Lord? It is not possible for most of us to go into all the world, but this does not exclude us from teaching the gospel to every creature within our own small world. We must begin somewhere! Jesus told His disciples to begin in Jerusalem. I believe we are to begin where we are . . . in our homes and out to our neighborhood.

The Greatest Commandment

God has told us emphatically in both the Old and the New Testaments:

> You shall love the Lord your God with all your heart, with all your soul, and with all your mind. This is the first and greatest commandment. And the second is like it: "You shall love your neighbor as yourself" (Matthew 22:37-39).

These verses teach that we are to love God first (with everything within us) then this love will cause us to love our neighbors as ourselves. Since we have established that everyone we meet is our neighbor, then it follows that we will love that person just as we do ourselves.

Loving Ourselves

A servant must learn to love himself. It is very important that we value ourselves the way God values us (He knows every hair on our heads and has engraved us on the palm of His hands).

When once we value ourselves, we are free to forget ourselves in service to others. A person who does not love himself will fret about himself and think about himself constantly. A person who understands God's estimate of himself will have a wholesome self-esteem which reaches out to bless the lives of others.

When we love our neighbors as ourselves we will look for ways to help and serve. We will listen and sense needs — we will treat our neighbors as Christ would treat them. We will be thoughtful and caring neighbors with servant hearts.

Who Is My Neighbor?

He may live next door —
He may be an old person, sick or a bore.
Speak kindly, treat gently, clothe warmly or feed,
But somehow, or someway, take care of his need!

— Mary Oler

The Jesus Lifestyle

Sometimes we may not admit that separation from our neighbors may be due to separation from God. Have you ever thought about that?

We need to make ourselves right with God before we can have a right relationship with others. We must learn to love God with all our hearts, minds and spirits. In order to show the love of God to our neighbors, we must be filled to the brim and overflowing with that love.

Christ came into the world to make a brotherhood of mankind. He is, in fact, our elder Brother. He taught us *how* to love. He taught us the real meaning of service. We have never really lived until we have learned to imitate the lifestyle of Jesus.

Trends in lifestyles come and go, but no one person ever gave Himself more freely, or lost Himself more fully in service than our blessed Jesus.

He taught us not only to love our neighbors, He taught (and demonstrated) love for our enemies as well.

> "You have heard that it was said, 'You shall love your neighbor and hate your enemy.' "

> "But I say to you, Love your enemies, bless those who curse you, do good to those who hate you

and pray for those who spitefully use you and
persecute you," (Matthew 5:43,44).

Why?

"that you may be sons of your Father in heaven;
for He makes His sun rise on the evil and on the
good, and sends rain on the just and on the un-
just" (Matthew 5:45).

God has given us free choice. We can except or reject His teachings to love God first, our neighbor second, and ourselves last. We must make that decision on our own.

Should we choose the selfish path, we will often find ourselves alone and miserable.

The path of service is not always a pathway free of hardship, strain and trouble. It is often a path involving jeopardy and risk, but it provides more light, joy and genuine fulfillment than any other way.

As we grow in Christ, we will find ourselves giving up more and more of our own "so called" rights. What will be the results? Finding ourselves and discovering "what life is all about."

He who finds his life will lose it, and he who loses
his life for My sake will find it (Matthew 10:39).

We will eventually discover what Christ has been showing us all along. Genuine love will cause us to seek the forgiveness of our enemies, which will result in peace between the two of us.

Do you have a neighbor who hates and despises you? Bless him, do good to him and pray for him. This is the Jesus lifestyle.

Your Mission Field

You have something to do in your community which nobody else can do. Your community, your neighborhood, is your mission field for Christ.

As I began preparations for writing this book, there were many things I wanted to say, yet I felt very inadequate. It is hard to put into words the feelings of the heart. I felt I needed the help of the Lord. The only thing I could do was to put myself and what I wanted to say, into God's hands and let Him do the work through me.

This is probably the way most of us feel about working in this great mission field so close to home. Very inadequate.

Too Close

Oh, now, Lord look here!
If it were some big task
You gave me to do . . .
Some courageous, dangerous task
Like crossing the ocean . . .
Some sacrificial act like
Leaving all my loved ones
To carry the Gospel to some
Lost and dark Continent . . .

Why, if that was the case
I'd go gladly.
What a challenge that would be!
But here? In *this* neighborhood?
Lord, my neighbors know me too well.
And I'm afraid I know too much
About them too.
Lord, You've really got to be
kidding!

You're asking me to tell them
About You?
We're just too close
My neighbors and me.
Just ask, Lord, just ask . . .
Send me anywhere.
Not here.
Some other place would
Be better for me.

— Judy Miller

Let Your Light So Shine

God wants to live out His love life through us. Let us as Christian women find out His plan for our lives and live therein. It is only our reasonable service that we yield our lives to Him and let Him work through us (Romans 12:1).

... for it is God who works in you both to will and to do for His good pleasure. Do all things without murmuring and disputing, that you may become blameless and harmless children of God without fault in the midst of a crooked and perverse generation, among whom you shine as lights in the world (Philippians 2:13-15).

Maybe you don't live in a crooked and perverse neighborhood ... certainly I don't. In fact, just the opposite is true. I have some of the finest neighbors in the world. Many are trying to work out the will of the Lord in their lives and are good examples to me.

Just a Little Thing

It was just a little thing,
So said my neighbor there.
Just a fifteen minute chat,
But it lifted my despair

Doing things for others —
That's how her days were spent.
To her they seemed like nothing,
But oh, how much they meant.

I know not her source of strength;
Yet one thing was plain.
Love was her motive;
There was no thought of gain.

I'm sure she never wrote a book,
Or saw her name in lights;
But I have heard her pray,
Keeping vigil with long nights.

She never flew around the world;
She owned no real estate.
Few would know her name,
But God would call her great.

— Author Unknown

"She has done what she could," Jesus said about the woman who poured a sweet ointment on His head. If all of us would make up our mind to do whatever we can to help another, there would be a "world" of difference in our world. God expects us to use whatever we have at our disposal in His service.

"What is that in your hand?" God asked Moses. He asks us the same question. What do you have that is uniquely yours to give and bless others?

Our acts of service are like seeds which we plant in the garden of our neighbor's hearts. Seeds seem like such tiny, insignificant things but when planted, they burst into beautiful bloom. Although God sends the sunshine, I often think that God needs us as sunbeams to help His harvest develop and thrive.

I Planted a Garden

I planted a garden within my heart
And tended it with care,
And now so many happy thoughts
I find are blooming there.

First there's a row of sunny smiles
And in between a kiss,
And in my garden now I find
There's love and happiness.

A golden sunshine ever bright
Helps kindly deeds to grow,
And special seeds of friendliness
Are all the kind I sow.

The rain is only silver threads
And every smile's a rose,
That never wilts and never dies
But grows and grows and grows.

To keep the garden within my heart
A very special one,
I pluck the seeds of hate and scorn
And plant a row of fun.

A seed of joy and a seed of love
And a kindly thought each day,
Always enough so that I might have
A part I can give away.

So that every flower I choose to pick
Will blossom from the start,
And make me proud of the things I grow
In the garden of my heart.

— Garnett Ann Schultz

Do you recall going into your garden and finding a little flower or plant growing there which you had not planted? Where did it come from?

It came from your neighbor's seeds which had been carried by the wind from her garden to yours. In much the same way our loving actions and deeds blow into the lives of our friends and neighbors. Let us cultivate our spirits with godly acts, thoughts and actions so that our neighbors will be blessed.

The Aging Servant

A beautiful thought is expressed in Psalm 92:12-15:

> The righteous shall flourish
>   like a palm tree,
> He shall grow like a cedar
>   in Lebanon.
> Those who are planted in
>   the house of the Lord
> Shall flourish in the courts
>   of our God.
> They shall still bear fruit in
>   old age;
> They shall be fresh and
>   flourishing,
> To declare that the Lord is upright;
>   He is my rock, and there is
> no unrighteousness in
>   Him.

Like me, you may be rapidly approaching the age when, more than likely, we will be referred to as "senior citizens." This Psalm has great hope and beauty. It tells us that if we are righteous we shall be planted in the house of the Lord, flourishing and still bearing fruit — even in old age!

This is enormously comforting. It makes us look forward to

old age rather than dreading it. It means we can look forward to years of serving the Lord in fresh and vital ways. We can develop even more vigorously in servanthood.

Like an evergreen tree, we can grow sweeter, more mellow — more alert to the needs presented right in our own neighborhoods.

Ways to Encourage in Your Neighborhood:

A servant mind will cause us to reach out to our neighbors — to encourage as the flame reaches out for iron, embracing it and making a difference.

Here is a list of some things we can do for the glory of God on the street where we live:

1. Speak kind, cheerful and comforting words to your neighbors, especially when they are sad and downcast.

    > Anxiety in the heart of a man causes depression,
    > but a good word makes it glad (Proverbs 12:25).

    Are you a refreshing Christian as Onesiphorus was to Paul? 2 Timothy 1:16 relates that Onesiphorus often refreshed Paul and was not ashamed of Paul's chains. He deliberately sought him out until he found him. Many of our neighbors could stand some refreshing, comforting words.

2. Sympathize with one who has lost a loved one. Do anything to be of help. Someone has said, "He who sees a need and waits to be asked, is as unkind as if he had refused it." The greatest thing we can do for a neighbor who has suffered loss is to be there for them. Your presence speaks far more than words.

3. Bake a pie, cake or casserole and take it to a sick or lonely neighbor. Remember one who cares . . . shares.

4. Take a meal to a new-comer or invite her into your home while she is moving in. Some of the best friends you may ever make may be someone who has just moved in near you. All of us can remember how happy it made us to have someone come by to greet us and welcome us to the new neighborhood.

5. Make a telephone call just to say, "I'm thinking of you," or to say, "I'm grateful for what you did or said." All of us love receiving calls from friends or neighbors who call on impulse . . . just because!

6. Write a note of encouragement. Make your own "sunshine notes." We don't have to buy expensive greeting cards. The notes which bring the greatest joy are hand-written notes, penned from the heart. Learn to write in calligraphy and your notes will be more precious than any card manufactured and copied by the thousands. It's the personal touch that counts. Be an original!
7. Share your gifts and talents: Sewing, handicrafts, art work, baking, writing, reading the Bible or other inspirational literature. Examine your natural gifts. Sometimes you find out what they are by serving others. God has called each one of us to serve in a unique way.
8. Keep a busy mother's children in your home or go to hers and keep them so she can get out awhile. While you are there, do a little light housekeeping, or leave a pie or cookies. Remember that service is love in working clothes.
9. Call on the elderly and shut-ins. Visit nursing homes if possible. Wash the feet of those who cannot. Our older friends are a divine gift to be cherished. There are many lonely people. Tell them how much they are missed. Our elderly people are our most neglected group.
10. Help a new mother with her baby or help with the older children.
11. Refrain from unloading your ailments or problems on your neighbors, but listen carefully and prayerfully while they tell you theirs. We converted a lady who formerly lived across the street from us primarily because she needed someone to listen to her.
12. Make short calls on the ill, taking a meal and helping in any way. "Blessed are those who give without remembering and take without forgetting."
13. Remember your neighbors when a child graduates or marries.
14. Share your own joy about being a Christian. Help them to know the Lord's plan for their lives. "Not that we have dominion over your faith, but are helpers of your joy" (2 Corinthians 1:24).
15. Invite your neighbors to the services. Provide a way for them or their children. You never know what might come from a single invitation. Many times a parent has been brought to the Lord after seeing the difference in his or her child when they were exposed to faithful teaching.

16. Share a tract on a particular subject. It might not do any good, but then again, it might.
17. Share your faith in times of stress or trouble. Many people are living without hope. When they see how you handle your problems, it will cause them to ask questions. But sanctify the Lord God in your hearts, and always be ready to give a defense to everyone who asks you for a reason for the hope that is in you, with meekness and fear (1 Peter 3:15).
18. Invite your neighbors into your home for a Bible study. Cultivate an open home. Develop a spirit of hospitality. Be more relaxed about the appearance of your house. If we are not ashamed of the gospel, we will be open to having people into our homes for Bible studies.
19. An individual or couple may be invited into your home for a private study. You may want to use the Open Bible method or the Jule Miller video tapes. Whatever you use, study from God's book!
20. Gather the neighborhood children into your home or backyard for a Bible class. I have done this and it is a blessing.
21. Bring a friend with you to Ladies' Bible Class. She might come to this class when she wouldn't come to any other service of the church.
22. Encourage young people to stay strong in their faith. Youth may often be reached easier than adults. Children's hearts are fertile soil.
23. Never be afraid to apologize for any wrong you have done. We all feel better once we have confessed a shortcoming and who of us hasn't made mistakes? That's why there are erasers on pencils!
24. Show interest in your neighbor's house and gardens. Everyone likes a little praise. We all work hard on our houses and yards and, when someone notices, it is a great booster.
25. Don't covet your neighbor's material possessions. What we have is far more priceless. Let us share with them the real wealth.
26. Make every effort to avoid participating in gossip. The Christian does not engage in gossip and slander. When we hear an unkind word said about another, we can be like Christ by saying something kind.

The Tongue

A quick whisper in the dark,
  A couple of turns around the park
"I'll tell you what Jane told me,
  Sue said, Jim said . . . was seen by Mary Lee"

Throw a pebble into a pond,
  Watch the ripples move on and on
Gossip repeated, be it false or fact,
  Can never, never be brought back.

The tongue, a small fire — oh, my yes
  But what destruction and distress;
A careless word dropped here and there
  Sputters and flickers, then quickly flares.

Small faults, like flames whipped by a wind
  Soon mount into a major sin,
Told and retold, self-righteous pride,
  Another victim crucified.

          — Author Unknown

27. Remember that unlovely people need more love than others. The neighbors we avoid the most are usually the ones who actually need us most. People are hungry for encouragement. Sometimes people act ugly because somewhere along the way they have been treated badly. As Christian servants we can restore their faith in themselves.
28. Serve in your local P.T.A. or other community organizations where your Christian influence may be felt. A word of caution here: A woman who is rearing small children needs to examine her priorities. After looking carefully and prayerfully at the amount of time you have to give to husband, children, home and personal Bible study, decide whether you have enough time to give to your community. If you honestly do not have time, relax and do not feel guilty. Many women have little to do except gad about from one neighbor's house to another. This is *not* the kind of service we are speaking about. The Bible warns about being a busybody in the affairs of others. Let us strive for a happy balance. Be like Mary and choose the better part and say "no" to other things.

Proverbs 3:27 and 28 sums up what we have emphasized in this lesson:

> Do not withhold good from
> those to whom it is due,
> When it is in the power of
> your hand to do so.
> Do not say to your neighbor,
> Go, and come back,
> And tomorrow I will give it,
> When you have it with you.

Our neighbors are God's children. Christ died for them, too. As our love for God grows so will our love for our neighbors. Jesus came to show us God and to demonstrate that love is best shown in acts of good-will and service.

We all have good intentions of being better servants on our block. Opportunities are presented to us every day. We need only look around to find them.

Closed Doors

I saw a door
And meant to go
Within the room someday.

I looked around and marked the ground
Lest I forget the way.

When I returned
All was the same
Excepting
Where before a light had been
No light was seen
And God had closed the door.

— Author Unknown

CHAPTER TEN

SOMETHING TO THINK ABOUT TODAY

1. What is your definition of a neighbor?
2. What do you think Jesus meant when He told the Lawyer to "go and do likewise?"
3. Name the three-fold aspects of the great commandment as found in Matthew 22:37-39.
4. Why is it so important that we value ourselves? How does God value us?
5. We need to make ourselves right with _____ before we can have a right relationship with _____.
6. True or False?
   A. The path of service is free of hardship, strain and troubles.
   B. It provides more fulfillment than any other way.
   C. As we grow in Christ, we will gain more and more of "our rights."
   D. Genuine love will cause us to ask our enemies to straighten up their lives.
   E. If a neighbor hates us, we are to hate him in return.
7. How would you define "reasonable service?"
8. It is _____ who works in _____, both to _____ and to _____ for His good pleasure (Philippians 2:13).
9. Discuss the comparison of planting seeds and that of acts of service.
10. As we grow older, what happens to one who has spent a life time developing the servant's spirit?
11. Twenty-eight suggestions for service are listed in this chapter. Pick out five suggestions which you believe are ways in which you can shine best.
12. Memorize Proverbs 3:27 and 28 and share it with a neighbor today.

CHAPTER 11

A HOME LOVING SPIRIT

Many women are floundering around in the dark trying to find where their ministries lie. They are thoroughly frustrated, wondering if their God given talents are to be hidden forever. They soon find themselves listening to every source but God. No wonder they are confused!

God wants us to live in *His* plan — so we pray for wisdom and strength to fit our plans into His will (and not the other way around). Sometimes we plan our lives the way we want to live them. Then we seek God's approval. We need to allow God to direct our lives through His Word.

God's Plan in the Beginning

In the beginning woman was created to be a "help meet" for her husband — one very suitable and needed — one who would complete what he lacked.

> And the Lord God said, "It is not good that the man should be alone; I will make him an help meet for him" (Genesis 2:18). (KJV)

In the New Testament, Paul, guided by the Holy Spirit, wrote in 1 Timothy 5:14:

> Therefore I desire that the younger widows marry, bear children, manage the house, give no opportunity to the adversary to speak reproachfully.

Titus 2:4 and 5 admonishes women to "teach the young women to be sober, to love their husbands, to love their children, to be discreet, chaste, keepers at home, good, obedient to their own husbands, that the word of God be not blasphemed."

This does not mean that single and childless women are outside the will of God. He has a plan in His word for everyone. From these passages of Scripture, we learn that a woman's *primary* role is in the home where she may love her husband, children and be keepers at home. The most sublime goal a woman can attain is having her entire family believe home is the best place in the world.

Someone has said:

> "No nation, no church, and no home can stand, without the woman there, as the molder of all that is excellent, refined and beautiful." An ancient proverb reads: "if there be righteousness within the individual, there will be happiness in the home; if there is happiness in the home there will be harmony in the nation; if there is harmony in the nation, there will be peace in the world."

The influence of a good woman is more far-reaching than can be estimated. God has always blessed the faithful service of a woman "that fears the Lord" (Proverbs 31:30).

A Woman's Position

> So God created man in His own image; in the image of God He created him; male and female He created them (Genesis 1:27).

God created male and female in His own image and both have equal value in His sight. Yet God placed man in the home as its head, and the woman in the home as its heart.

> But I want you to know that the head of every man is Christ, the head of woman is man, and the head of Christ is God (1 Corinthians 11:3).

Man is subordinate to Christ, just as wives are to be subordinate to their husbands. Just because wives are commanded to be submissive to their husbands does not mean they are inferior to them. It was never in the mind of God that a husband be a tyrant or the wife be a doormat. To be submissive is a loving, caring attitude. When a woman truly loves and trusts her husband she will be happy to remain in the position in which God has placed her.

Both men and women are called upon to have a yielding, submissive spirit to their God. This gives them purpose and infinite joy. Our primary purpose is to serve and glorify God with all our hearts . . . "submitting to one another in the fear of God" (Ephesians 5:21).

A Woman's Self-Worth

It must be remembered that before Christ came, women were considered inferior beings. Women could not have property rights; they could not be educated. Indeed many were considered too obtuse to be taught.

Women were down-graded and subjected to much injustice and unfairness. When Jesus came, He set women free to be their best selves. He gave them opportunities to know their self-worth and to grow and develop as individuals with talents and abilities of their own.

Many of the women who were "fellow servants of Christ" such as Dorcus, Phoebe, Lydia and Priscilla had great abilities and they were commended through the gospel for their loving acts of service.

Lois and Eunice — grandmother and mother of Timothy — set before us great examples of the importance of godly training in the home. They shared their knowledge of Bible truths and imparted this to young Timothy's heart until his faith grew to be as normal as living and breathing. His young heart and mind were fed upon the Gospel in his impressionable years in the home.

As a result of Christ's coming and Paul's teaching, women were elevated and esteemed highly for their work's sake. It is precious to read passages such as Galatians 3:25-28 and realize our worth in Christ Jesus:

> But after faith has come, we are no longer under a tutor. For you are all sons of God through faith in Christ Jesus. For as many of you as were baptized into Christ have put on Christ. There is neither Jew nor Greek, there is neither slave nor free, there is neither male nor female; for you are all one in Christ Jesus.

I'll never worry about inequality again! I know I am important to Christ. When I am baptized into Christ, I am in Christ and that makes all the difference. I'll never lose a moment's sleep over women's liberation. I *am* liberated in Christ, for Christ had set me free from the law of sin and death.

A Woman's Highest Role

A woman's highest role in the church and home is service and love.

A woman's full time service is to love, whether in the church or the family. "Divine service conducted here three times daily" is a motto placed in many a woman's home.

Paul wrote in Galatians 6:9:

> And let us not grow weary while doing good, for in due season we shall reap if we do not lose heart. Therefore as we have opportunity, let us do good to all, especially to those who are of the household of faith.

It is so easy for any of us to become weary in well doing for lack of encouragement. "And let us consider one another in order to stir up love and good works." Where are our older women when it comes to stirring up our younger women to love and good works?

"Church Work"

There are untold opportunities in the church of our Lord for women to render service. A woman is certainly not limited to her home for her sphere of work. A woman's work is as far-reaching as her abilities and talents take her — but a woman's work for the Lord naturally begins in the home.

When we speak of a woman's role in the church we usually refer only to work we do apart from our homes as "church work." But I think it is about time we began to reassess the meaning of "church work." "Church work" is not even a biblical term.

I believe a woman who has been given a home — and one or a dozen children has much of her "church work" established for her. The more children — the more demands on her time and energies. Whatever time is left over, she should and must give to others. We might refer to this as "other church activities."

All our work, as women (assuming it is good and honest work) is to be considered "church work." We are the church, and wherever we are at work, the church is at work. A woman must be very careful that she doesn't become caught up in so many outside church activities that she neglects those precious souls for whom she is most responsible.

We cannot do the world's work, but we can do our own. Someone has said: "A woman who creates and sustains a home, makes a man feel loved and understood, and under whose hands children grow up to be strong and pure men and women is a creator second only to God."

A woman doesn't need to feel pressured to compete with a man. Man has his work and woman has hers. Each is wonderfully equipped to do the work that God intends for us to do. It's important to find our sphere of service and be delighted with the health and ability to do it.

Home should be a place of peace and refuge for everyone who lives there. It is primarily the woman who makes it that way. For young mothers in particular, "church work" means "home work."

Women who are wives and mothers have the highest and most noble responsibilities and privileges placed in their hands. The responsibilities are great, but may I add very joyous. To be able to be the helpmeet and companion of a godly man, to raise his children; to guide and keep the home is our sweetest privilege, our highest calling.

Ruth Graham said in a magazine article many years ago: "God has placed us as homemakers in our homes by divine appointment!" I have thought about this many times when things seemed mundane and dreary and remembered that God placed me in the home to work and do His good will.

I personally feel that a woman serves best from her home. I believe this is her biblical role. For those women who *must* help make the living for the family or at least to supplement it, I have only admiration and respect. I shall always encourage such a woman never to feel guilty. Even though a woman must work for a living, there is still much work to be done at home.

I believe we should use all our minutes, hours and days to the glory of the heavenly Father. This is what we were placed on earth to do. Everything we accomplish no matter how small, should be an offering to Him who has done so much for us.

Our daily work is a part of God's plan for us and a very appropriate part. The woman who keeps busy and interested in serving others by the work of her hands is a happy woman. She has no business and certainly no time to brood and feel sorry for herself. "The fullest life is the one emptied for the sake of others."

When we as Christian women can clearly see the picture of God's love as focused on the cross, then you and I can understand our roles. We can respond to this love with trust, serenity and with a reliance that colors all our activities.

So much has been written and said by the feminists about a woman's rights that some women feel guilty staying at home and taking care of the members of their own home. Baking bread, sewing small seams and reading Bible stories have almost become a thing of the past.

Choices

Joshua declared in Joshua 24:15:

> And if it seems evil to you to serve the Lord, choose for yourselves this day whom you will serve, whether the gods which your fathers served that were on the other side of the River, or the gods of the Amorites, in whose land you dwell. But as for me and my house, we will serve the Lord.

This is a firm declaration of faith on Joshua's part in behalf of the entire family. Who makes the decisions about which direction little children are going? Who decides what values and character traits will be taught in the home? Who sets the examples of dedicated God fearing living? It is the mother and father in the home. Early in the marriage of two people they choose whom they will serve whether it be the pleasures of this life, or the riches in Christ.

We as mothers and wives must make a daily decision to *serve* the Lord! "Choose you this day." Why daily? Because day after day, Satan tries to get *at us* with all his might, hoping to defeat our commitment to the Lord. He is extremely subtle, endeavoring with every trick at his disposal to make us believe one lie after another. We must be very strong to see through his devices — to find strength to overcome temptations which are presented daily.

God wants to rule in the hearts of every member of the family. In a very real sense, the mother and father in the home must make the daily decision to love each other, love their children, and to train and guide them consistently and patiently in biblical principles. Albert Schwartzer once said: "There are only three ways to teach a child. The first is by example, the second is by example, and the third is by example." This is so true.

When we say "as for me and my house, we will serve the Lord" we are making a promise before God that we will not put anything or anybody above our service to our Heavenly Father. Little children, even though very young, cannot help but sense the love and faith in Mother and Daddy when Christianity is lived out on a daily basis.

We can bestow no greater heritage on children than to leave them a strong faith in Jehovah God. Christ must be placed supreme in our lives daily: In all the little tasks — all the little decisions, all the little discussions, all the little actions, all the little songs, all the little smiles, all the little sharings, all the little tears and all the little choices. As a result our children will discover for themselves that here is a family which has chosen to serve the Lord.

Then, and only then, will we come to the day when our children will say to us as Israel said to Joshua:

... We also will serve the Lord, for He is our God.

Do you want to rear children who will become godly servants and active participants in the kingdom of Christ? Then it is absolutely imperative that we "choose this day whom we will serve."

Full Time Service

A woman serves the Lord *best* when she serves her family *first*. There are many opportunities for Christian service but a woman's work naturally *begins* in the home. We who are older women are instructed to teach the younger women to be "keepers at home." I believe this means we are to be the organizer of all home activities. No one can do the work which needs to be done in the home better than the wife and mother in that home. For every role on earth there is only one to fill it. No one can fill our roles as we can.

God must have a special place in His heart for women who love to stay at home — not because we must, but because it is our choice. As Longfellow said: "Homekeeping hearts are happiest."

A Woman's World

> And God is able to make all grace abound toward you, that you, always having all sufficiency in all things, have an abundance for every good work (2 Corinthians 9:8).

Think with me for a moment. What areas of responsibility make up a woman's world? We must be many things to many people. We must be a woman, wife, mother, daughter, sister, friend, neighbor and homemaker. Think of all a woman does in her home alone!

She is housekeeper, nursemaid, cook, laundress, dishwasher, food buyer, gardener, manager, chauffeur, dietitian, bookkeeper, dressmaker, religious instructor, teacher, family correspondent and much more.

The world tells me I need to go outside my home to be fulfilled. Help! If I were any more fulfilled I would explode! The value of basic importance is being faithful to a responsibility. Failure to fulfill responsibilities will bring disappointment and grief.

What are my responsibilities then? What has God placed in my personal keeping? The world says, "You have a responsibility to yourself!" If I understand my Bible correctly, I am responsible first to God!

Second, I am responsible to other human beings, especially those placed in my keeping. When I seek the good of others, my family included, I have met my responsibility. Serving and helping others gives me a satisfaction and self-fulfillment that no amount of self-indulgence could every bring. Self-fulfillment is like happiness . . . it is not something one may obtain by searching for it. It is a product of giving one's self in service to others.

I am thankful God's Word has defined our role as women . . . servants!

The longer I live, the deeper I believe that we as women are called to full time service for the Lord. Men are too, but women are often given a warmer nature; a more compassionate spirit. If this is so, we need to spread warmth and love upon all those who come into our sphere of influence — *beginning with those who live in our homes.*

Let us make our homes Christian homes!

We should never underestimate the power of Christian

service in the home. The churches of tomorrow will be made up of the children we have reared today.

If you are a single woman who plans to marry some day, my plea for you is to begin right now with the dreams and visions you have for your future children. Become all you know God wants you to be, but above all, plan to marry a Christian man! He will be that daddy to whom Paul advised, "Bring your children up in the nurture and training of the Lord."

We need to understand that the place we are standing *at the present time* is Holy Ground. When we recognize this to be true, we as Christian wives and mothers will *turn aside to see* what God wants us to do.

CHURCH OF CHRIST, EAST FRAYSER
2285 FRAYSER BLVD.
MEMPHIS, TN 38127
(901) 357-7444

CHAPTER ELEVEN

SOMETHING TO THINK ABOUT TODAY

1. In the beginning woman was created to be a _____. What does this mean?
2. When all is said and done, what is the reason that older women are to teach the younger women?
3. What is the true value of submissiveness?
4. True or false? Only women are called to be submissive.
5. Name several women who were commended through the gospel for their loving acts of service.
6. What were the names of the two women who were most responsible for Timothy's godly training in the home?
7. In what way can we say that Christian women are liberated?
8. What is a woman's highest role in the church and home?
9. True or False?
    A. There are few opportunities for women to serve in the church.
    B. A woman is limited to the home for her sphere of work.
    C. A woman's work naturally begins in the home.
    D. We are the Church, and wherever we are at work, the Church is at work.
10. Why must a woman be careful about being involved in too many outside church activities?
11. Discuss reasons why a woman doesn't need to feel pressured to compete with a man.
12. Home should be a place of _____ and _____.
13. Why is a woman happiest when she keeps busy and interested in serving others?
14. What do we mean when we say "As for me and my house, we will serve the Lord?"
15. What is the greatest heritage we can bestow upon our children?
16. What areas of responsibility make up a woman's world?
17. The place where we are standing is _____ _____. We need to _____ _____ _____ _____ what God wants us to do.

CHAPTER TWELVE

A JOYFUL SPIRIT

Do you remember when you were a child and you awakened in the morning with a keen sense of adventure? You couldn't wait to hop out of bed, so eager were you to see what the day might hold. Anticipation, excitement, wonder — all were there. This was your new day and you didn't want to miss any part of it!

Wouldn't it be great if we as grownups could recapture even a small part of that spirit of adventure?

Wouldn't it be marvelous if we couldn't wait to start each new day?

We can awaken in the morning with visions of tasks to be done, people to be faced, a work schedule to fulfill, and all hope can die before we have even put our feet on the floor. Even pulling the covers over our heads doesn't take away the gloomy sense of dread. What has happened to our sense of adventure, our love for living, our quest for learning and participating in new ventures? Where have all our wonder and zest gone?

If we awaken with the positive thought that God has given us this new day, rich with promise, then our attitudes and feelings about the day can be radically changed. With the transformation which God is continually making in our hearts and souls, we can arise with joy and hope in our hearts. We will never doubt for one moment that God is not here.

The Day Returns

The day returns
And brings us the petty round
Of irritating concerns and duties.
Help us to play the man!
Help us to perform them
With laughter and kind faces.

Let cheerfulness abound with industry.
Give us to go blithely on our business
All this day.

> Bring us to our resting beds
> Weary and content,
> And undishonored,
> And grant us in the end
> The gift of sleep.
>
> — Robert Louis Stevenson

A Joyful Heart

Yes, we need to serve the Lord with Joy!

> A merry heart makes a cheerful countenance, but by sorrow of heart the spirit is broken (Proverbs 15:13).

A joyful heart will free the spirit. Think of Paul and Silas singing songs at midnight in the Philippian jail. Their bodies might have been imprisoned but their spirits were free and soaring.

They were really serving the Lord with a joyful spirit. If they can do it, so can we. Paul, writing to the Roman Christians prayed:

> That I may come unto you with joy by the will of God, and may together with you, be refreshed (Romans 15:32).

A joyful nature refreshes the spirits of others. It is a delight to be around people who are full of joy and peace — a radiance which can only be attributed to the joy within.

Brighten Your Corner

> Have you noticed the great difference
> Between the people you meet?
> Some are as sunshiny as a handful of
> Forget-me-nots.
> Others come on like frozen mackerel.
> A cheery comforting nurse can help
> Make a hospital stay bearable.
> An upbeat secretary makes visitors
> Glad they came to see you.
> Every corner of the world has

Its clouds, gripers, complainers,
And pains in the neck —
Because many people have yet
To learn that honey works better
Than vinegar.
You're in control of your small corner
Of the world.
Brighten it . . .
You can.

— Author unknown

An Atmosphere of Joy

One of the most precious gifts we can give to other people (and especially the members of our own household) is a habit of joy and gladness.

There's something about being around a woman who is cheerful and joyful. She gives one a lift for the whole day. A woman of this nature creates the kind of atmosphere around her by the radiant, cheerful attitude that exuberates from her personality.

When a woman has a loving, joyous, personal relationship with her God, she is bound to spill some of it out on every person she meets. She can't help herself. It's as natural as the sun sending out its beams. We need to let the "Son" shine into our hearts so that our dispositions will be sunny and joyful.

Children can teach us a lot about joy, fun and enthusiasm. They never hold grudges for long. It takes so little to make a child happy. Simple, ordinary pleasures captivate them — their little eyes, sparkling with delight and wonder cause us to be joyful "way down under" as well.

A mother with a joyful spirit can literally transform the atmosphere around her. When she laughs, the children want to laugh with her. On the other hand, if she is cranky and cross — watch out!

Our own lives settle the rhythm of the home just as the heartbeat or the pulse settles the rhythm of the heart. The mother and wife in the home is truly the "heartbeat" of home. It has often been said that home is where the heart is. If a mother is the "heartbeat" of home, that means she is the pulsating, vibrating, throbbing force that gives the home it's continuing life and power.

Serve the Lord With Gladness

> Make a joyful shout to the Lord,
>   all you lands!
> Serve the Lord with
>   gladness;
> Come before His presence
>   with singing.
>
> — (Psalm 100:1,2)

We are to serve the Lord with *gladness*. In so doing, we will be naturally loving, naturally joyous, naturally peaceful, naturally patient with others — sharing all the wonderful fruit produced by the Holy Spirit.

"Come before His presence with singing." Tasks seem sweeter and lighter when one has a song in her heart. As we sing, the little tasks which are so irritable to us become emblems of "the sacrifice of praise" we can humbly offer Him. No one except our families may hear our song, but if they are blessed then the song is gilded with glory.

Hearts cannot be sad and troubled long when we have a song on our lips and Christ's joy in our hearts. Does the song bring the joy or does the joy produce the song? I guess we'll never know but either way — it's precious to have a song.

God warned the people of punishment in Deuteronomy 28:47, because "they served not the Lord with joyfulness and gladness of heart." A heart out of tune with God cannot sing — a heart in tune with God *must* sing. Joy is praise released and freed. We who love the lord with thankful hearts can no more refrain from singing than eating, drinking or sleeping.

God has been wonderfully kind. This motivates us to serve with jubilence, expecting good. The Lord surprises us daily with unexpected gifts. We need only look up — anticipating He will send them. Our days would be much more joyful if we looked at all our tasks as God given privileges to serve.

A Merry Heart

Our words and the manner in which we express them have a much greater impact on our families than most of us realize. Often, we are kinder to strangers than we are to the dearest on earth to us. God did not intend for this to be true. Our words, if fitly spoken, are like "apples of gold in pictures of silver" (Proverbs 25:11).

Think what a merry or cheerful heart can do. "A merry heart does good like a medicine but a broken spirit dries up the bones" (Proverbs 17:22). We can mend a child's broken spirit by our cheerful words. This is a ministry, Ladies. Don't ever think of your service as insignificant.

Ripples on the water are so even, so harmonious. They are fun to watch because they bring a certain peace to the soul. In the same way joy and gladness bring harmony and peace to the lives of those around us.

"A happy face means a glad heart; a sad face means a breaking heart" (Proverbs 15:13). Ladies, lets put on happy faces around our families. No more long, sad faces – please! This should be easy because of our "happy faith." We have too many reasons to be glad.

I want you to do something for yourself right now. Smile! Yes, smile whether you are reading this lesson or studying in a classroom situation. Now, don't you feel better? And doesn't everyone around you *look* better?

"When a man is gloomy, everything seems to go wrong, when he is cheerful, everything seems right" (Proverbs 15:15). How true this is. How much smoother and sweeter things move along when everyone is happy, kind and thoughtful to others.

Just think of how much we can do for our families and others when we are expressing "the joy of the Lord."

Where does joy originate? Psalm 16:11 shows us where it may be obtained:

> You will show me the path of life;
> In Your presence is n fullness of joy;
> At your right hand are pleasures forevermore.

From the presence of God we obtain our joy; and thus fortified at His banquet table – we can spread "joyful feasts" before our families and friends.

An Exciting Adventure

"The trouble with life" someone has observed, "is that it is so *daily!*" That many would feel this way is certainly understandable. Life can tend to be tiresome, hum-drum, and full of the same old routines day after day. We make friends, we lose them, we get sick, and we get tired. Our children and our mates disappoint us. There doesn't seem to be much purpose in getting up in the first place just to go through the same dreary chores and see the same dreary people everyday . . . what a drag!

But not to the child of God! No, to those of us involved in living the Christian life, there is a different perspective. When God is in our day everything takes on another aspect; our days become charged with power and victorious living.

Everyday we can step out with God into an exciting new adventure! The Christian whose life is hid with God in Christ Jesus (Colossians 3:3) looks forward to everyday. The Bible tells us that God daily loads us with benefits (Psalm 68:19).

Yes, everyday is wonderful when God is in it. Though our day may be filled with sorrow, problems and anxieties, it can still be a day overflowing with joyful living, for God is in this day! "This is the day which the Lord has made. We shall be glad and rejoice in it" (Psalm 124:18).

The Joy of the Lord

Nehemiah 8:10 is one of my favorite verses: "Do not sorrow, for the joy of the Lord is your strength."

"My verse!" — I have written in the margins beside this verse in my Bible. Yes, how strong is the assurance, "The joy of the Lord is your strength."

Glad and joyful service begins in the morning as we arise to greet the young and old in our family circle.

We can heal a wounded, sore heart with soothing, comforting words; we can stop the tears in baby's eyes by a warm kiss and hug. We can lift our husband's troubled mood by our encouragement. We can reassure our children with tender, loving expressions — we can mend a teenager's spirit by cheerfulness.

I am sure the worthy woman of Proverbs 31 arose with a happy spirit to face a day of serving others, for it is said of her:

> She also rises while it is yet night, and provides
> food for her household . . .(Proverbs 31:15).

If we would only approach our daily work with a joyful attitude, how much better things would go. The greatest work we do is not in cleaning our houses or dusting the furniture. The greatest work is with people. The most significant work we do is giving ourselves away with joy and gratitude, and passing on to others a happy spirit.

In Proverbs 15:23 we read that "A word spoken in season is good." We need to pray that we will not withhold the kind word, the joyful thought. Many times we do not say anything and, in so doing, we rob people of a gift.

Kissing the Joy

> He who binds to himself a joy
> Does the winged life destroy;
> But he who kisses the joy as it flies
> Lives in eternity's sunrise.
> To see a world in a grain of sand
> And a heaven in a wild flower;
> Hold eternity in the palm of your hand
> And eternity in an hour.
>
> — William Blake

We hold so much joy in our hands. Until we give joy away, it remains a crushed butterfly, dead in our hands. It just lies there, destroyed. But when we send joy out to bless the lives of others, it is like "kissing the joy as it flies."

Enthusiastic Joy

Enthusiasm carries with it a strong meaning: "God in us."
The Christian woman serves energetically and enthusiastically with the strong power of the Lord.

> Therefore, my beloved brethren, be steadfast, immovable, always abounding in the work of the Lord, knowing that your labor is not in vain in the Lord (1 Corinthians 15:58).

The word "abounding" means to overflow; to be plentiful, to be filled. It comes from the Greek word *perisseuo* which means "to turn out abundantly for something." The child of God "abounds" in good works and service for the Lord who abundantly supplies all our needs. God has placed His treasure in earthen vessels. Paul tells us in 2 Corinthians 4:7, "that the excellence of the power may be of God and not of us."

The Lord rebuked the church at Sardis because her works were dead and lifeless, (without heart) (Revelation 3:1 and 2). A caring, enthusiastic spirit was totally missing from their works.

We have already learned that we are to do all our service *heartily* as to the Lord (Colossians 3:23). The word "heartily" implies we are to do our work with all our heart. We are to put "heart power" into it.

We are to "give ourselves over into" our work for our Savior. It is so easy to wear ourselves out in secular work or in pursuits for gain and profit. When we do so, we do not have the strength and energy (or heart) to serve and help others in the family of God.

I see this happen frequently among couples who are so busy pursuing careers and making a living, they have no time to make a *life* with each other. All their energy and pep is drained by the time they get home!

Often what happens then is that their children are not served through play, recreation and fun activities. Families like this soon lose their basic closeness. *Things* rather than time spent together become the criteria of their daily existence. The result? Broken hearts, broken homes. Couples can also lose their enthusiasm and zeal for each other's company when too much time and attention is spent in the pursuit of success.

Success is a happy father and mother growing happy children and building a Christian home! One should never equate happiness with accumulated fame, fortune or financial security. The most secure happy people are those who *serve one another in love*. God's men and women are to be zealous (enthusiastic) for good works, not worldly pleasures.

Happiness consists not in getting but in giving. The happiest people are those who go out of their way to bring happiness to others. This very minute we can be happy by sending up a little prayer for another. Make a telephone call today, greeting someone with "Good morning, isn't it a beautiful day?"

Someone has said, "We act as though comfort and luxury were the chief requirements in life, when all we need to make us really happy is something to be *enthusiastic* about."

Let us therefore dress ourselves in enthusiasm today and go forth to serve. We are told in God's Word that we must die daily — we must also *live* daily for others. To live only to serve is not a bad ambition, for those who live only for themselves will ultimately be bored and miserable, for self is a lonely company.

Ralph Waldo Emerson wrote: "Rings and jewels are not gifts, but apologies for gifts. The only gift is a portion of thyself."

They say that enthusiasm and joy are contagious. If this is true, let us "catch" it from the Lord who has put His power into earthen vessels.

The Women of the Bible

The women of the Bible ever served
As earnestly as we would serve today.
Dorcas was full of good works, we are told,
And almsdeed which she did along her way.

Lydia, seller of purple, filled her hours
With useful beauty; Anna served with prayer
And fasting as she moved with quiet grace
Among the dim aisles of the temple there.

While Martha had a privilege so great
And beautiful we all might envy her;
To serve the Master in one's small home
Should truly set the strongest heart astir.

So we would serve today in church and home,
And so we too would toil with dignity
Conscious of the great importance, Lord,
Of a woman's work when it is done for Thee.

— Author Unknown

CHAPTER 12

SOMETHING TO THINK ABOUT TODAY

1. We need to serve the Lord with _____.
2. A joyful nature _____ the _____ of others.
3. What is one of the most precious gifts we can give to others?
4. How can a joyful mother transform the atmosphere around her?
5. The mother and wife in the home is truly the _____ of home.
6. Why did God warn the people He would punish them in Deuteronomy 28:47?
7. Do you ever think about your words and the manner in which you express them? What kind of impact do words have upon a family?
8. Compare the difference between a merry heart and a broken spirit. (Proverbs 17:22).
9. What is the source of joy? Where may it be obtained?
10. Why is Psalm 124:18 such a universal, beloved verse?
11. In Nehemiah 8:10 is a formula for strength. What is it?
12. True or False?
    A. The greatest work we can do is cleaning and dusting.
    B. We can rob people of a gift by not saying anything.
    C. We need to keep our joy entirely to ourselves.
    D. Enthusiasm means "God in us."
    E. The word "abounding" means to overflow.
    F. The Lord praised the church at Sardis because her works were plentiful and performed from the heart.
13. What does the word "heartily" imply?
14. Why is it so easy for us to wear ourselves out in secular work?
15. We are told in God's word that we _____ _____ _____; we must also _____ _____ for others.
16. Enthusiasm and joy are _____.
17. Where can we "catch" enthusiasm and joy?

CHAPTER 13

A LOVING, COMPASSIONATE SPIRIT

The Christian's Motivation

> For you, brethren, have been called to liberty; only do not use liberty as an opportunity for the flesh, but through love serve one another (Galatians 5:13).

All acts of service should be motivated by love. We have no greater example than that which was given us by the dear Lord Jesus when He was here on earth. His life was constantly being emptied in service to others. His was the most loving, compassionate heart which ever beat. No one ever loved like Jesus — no one ever cared like He.

Before Jesus left the earth, He gave His disciples a description of the way He wanted them to live after His departure:

> A new commandment I give to you, that you love one another: as I have loved you, that you also love one another. By this all will know that you are my disciples, if you have love for one another (John 13:34,35).

They were to love one another with the same kind of unselfish love with which He had loved them. This is truly *agape* love. There are all kinds of motives for serving others, but if we "have not love, it becomes a sounding brass or a changing cymbal" (1 Corinthians 13:1).

The greatest of these will always be love.

Unconditional Love

Jesus had unconditional love for all men and women. He did not love them on the basis of merit or reputation. He loved them period! Jesus expected the best in people but He never demanded that they be perfect before He could love them. Jesus loved the unlovely and those who least deserved it.

He accepted them as they were, and His love caused them to become better. He saw what people could become. Regardless of their lifestyle, He loved them *anyway*. In John 13:1 we are told:

> Having loved His own who were in the world, He loved them to the end.

He loved them to the full extent. His love extends just as far for us today. What a different world it would be if all of us could only demonstrate love as He did.

Growing Love

Is thy crust of comfort failing?
  Rise and share it with a friend.
And through all the years of famine
  It shall serve thee to the end.

For the heart grows rich in giving
  And all its wealth is living grain.
Seed, which mildew in the garner
  Scattered, fill with gold the plain.

Is thy heart a living power?
  Self-entwined, its strength sinks low.
It can only live by living,
  And by serving, love will grow.

— The Kleinknecht Gems of
Thought Encyclopedia

How very different our love is from that of our Savior's. If folks are worthy, we might love them. If they behave and do things that are acceptable to us, then we love then. We love them if they are clean and have a good education. We are very favorable to those who show love for us. There are many reasons why we love, but none of them can ever measure up to the kind of love Jesus bestowed on others.

Compassionate Love

In Matthew 9:36 we read:

> But when He saw the multitudes, He was moved with compassion for them, because they were weary and scattered, like sheep having no shepherd.

Christ exemplified His compassionate spirit in a beautiful manner when He answered the question presented by the lawyer in Luke 10:29. "You shall love your neighbor as yourself" Jesus said. The lawyer, wishing to justify himself asked: "And who is my neighbor?"

Instead of answering the question directly, Jesus told the story of the good Samaritan. The Samaritan was not merely "good," he was "good" in a winsome sense. He went beyond that which was expected of him and performed heartfelt service of a lovely kind.

We remember the priest and the Levite had already passed on the other side. They had seen "a certain man" who had fallen among thieves, been stripped of his clothing, wounded and left for dead.

The Samaritan, however, had compassion on the wounded beaten up man. What does it mean to have compassion on someone?

The word "compassion" means deep sympathy. It means to "sorrow for another." This is the kind of winsome attitude the Samaritan had for the poor victim whom he had stumbled upon "by chance."

He showed his compassionate heart — his winsome tender spirit, in several ways:

1. He went to him.

   For the most part this is the first step. We must go where there is a need. How easy it is for us to pass by on the other side while someone else does the going.

2. He bandaged his wound.

   He saw the immediate need and took the first step. The man was wounded and bleeding, so he set to work without regard to the risk to himself. Suppose the robbers were still lurking in the background? He didn't give it a second thought, or if he did — he disregarded the idea. Here was someone who was hurting, someone who needed his aid — as simple as that.

3. **He poured oil and wine on his wounds.**
   He sought to alleviate his pain and heal his wounds with *what he had on hand*. He did not hold back but freely gave of what he possessed.
4. **He set him on his own animal.**
   The donkey, ass or mule (whatever) had been brought on the trip for his own use. Here we see the unselfish nature of the Samaritan who was willing to do without in order that this wounded man's burden might be lightened.
5. **He brought him to the inn.**
   This was truly going the second mile. Whether he was on his way to the inn or not, the Samaritan certainly went out of his way to bring the hurt man to a place where he could rest and heal.
6. **He took care of him.**
   All night long he watched over him and did not leave his side until the next day. He did not have to do this, but he did because he had a loving spirit.
7. **He gave the innkeeper money.**

> On the next day, when he departed, he took out two denarii, gave them to the innkeeper, and said to him, "Take care of him; and whatever more you spend, when I come again, I will repay you."

He went far beyond what most of us would have done. His duty was accomplished way back there on the Jericho road. However, the Samaritan *wanted* to assume responsibility for this wounded man. He saw the service through until the last possible moment.

The compassionate, tender spirit of the "good" Samaritan endears him to us. Compassion is greatly needed in this cold, calculating world. What will it take to *move* us as Jesus was "moved with compassion?" It may very well be that we, ourselves, are going to have to go through some hard times (when we are badly in need of compassion) before we will understand.

Love Is

> Love is an attitude — love is a prayer
> For a soul in sorrow or a heart in despair;
> Love is good wishes for the gain of another;
> Love suffers long with the fault of a brother;
> Love filleth the cup when the waters run dry;

> Love reaches as low as it reaches high;
> Seeks not her own at expense of another;
> Love honors God when it reaches our brother.
>
> — Author Unknown

Small Acts of Love

In Matthew 10:42 we read:

> And whoever gives one of these little ones only a cup of cold water in the name of a disciple, assuredly, I say to you, he shall by no means lose his reward.

Even the smallest of kind deeds, done for Jesus' sake, shall not go unrewarded.

William O. Paulsell said:

> Christ is in me when I give a cup of cold water to a thirsty man, when I listen sympathetically to one who is in trouble, when I reach out to someone who needs to be loved; in short when I become a person for others.

A Person for Others!

Yes, this was the ultimate description of our Lord. How wonderful it would be if each of us decided to be "a person for others." How differently we would live if this were the theme of our lives. One of our sweet Christian ladies, Ruth Mann, died recently at the age of 82. All of us who attended her funeral will remember the minister's statement concerning Ruth's life: "She served God and others." Could a finer tribute be given anyone?

> Often the most useful Christians are those who serve their master in small things. He never despises the day of small things, or else He would not hide His oaks in tiny acorns, or the wealth of a wheat field in bags of little seeds.
>
> — Author Unknown

Love One Another

> For this is the message that you heard from the beginning, that we should love one another (1 John 3:11).
>
> And this is His commandment: that we should believe on the name of His Son Jesus Christ and love one another, as He gave us commandment (1 John 3:23).
>
> Beloved, let us love one another, for love is of God; everyone who loves is born of God and knows God (1 John 4:7).
>
> Beloved, if God so loved us, we also ought to love one another (1 John 4:11).

I love those two words . . . "one another." The Scriptures are full of "one-another" verses.

Jesus told us that the law of life and love is summed up in these words:

> You shall love the Lord your God with all your heart, with all your soul, with all your strength, and with all your mind, and your neighbor as yourself (Luke 10:27).

And James added:

> If you really fulfill the royal law according to the Scripture, "You shall love your neighbor as yourself," you do well; (James 2:8).

Love Deeply

Love is a short word but can you think of a better word to describe service? To love means to care . . . to care deeply for another's good. Love is giving of ourselves — unreservedly, whole-heartedly, without hypocrisy.

Jesus came to show us how to love. His death on the cross was the highest form of love. The opening words of the song: "To love someone more dearly every day" strike a chord in our hearts. The reason why we do not love more dearly, is that we do not love more *deeply*. We have never realized the depths of life, especially the depths of love. Paul wrote in Ephesians 3:17-19:

> ... that Christ may dwell in your hearts through faith; that you being rooted and grounded in love, may be able to comprehend with all the saints what is the width and length and depth and height — to know the love of Christ which passes knowledge; that you may be filled with all the fullness of God.

The word "deep" means "extending a great way below the surface." Our love needs to go beyond that which we see on the surface of a person's life. The deeper our love plunges, the more intense will be the ripples and therefore the further our service will abound.

Our love is often shallow, without depth. We hold back, unwilling, hesitating to be involved. This is a superficial love, one that can never know real expression. God's love was far from being superficial.

> There's a wideness in God's mercy
> Like the wideness of the sea;
> There's a kindness in His justice,
> Which is more than liberty.
> For the love of God is broader
> Than the measure of a man's mind;
> And the heart of the Eternal
> Is most wonderfully kind.
>
> — Author Unknown

When God sent His only begotten Son, He caused an enormous Ripple on the waters of this world. And the ripples continue to surge outward from His eternal love to touch millions of lives to this day!

The Ministry of Listening

One of the ways we can cultivate a loving, compassionate spirit is by listening to other people. I call this the ministry of the "listening heart."

If you have people coming and going out of your house; calling on the telephone for counsel, comfort and consolation ... be glad! This may take a great deal of time, and sometimes, like me, you may wonder if you are accomplishing anything at all. There is no greater service than quietly listening, sympathizing and offering loving advice when necessary.

Sometimes I feel like the telephone is a great hindrance. Just about the time I get involved with a project, lesson preparation, or my quiet time, I might be interrupted by a telephone call. I have come to look upon such interruptions as God's opportunities for Christian service.

Often, before I lift up the receiver, I ask God to help me be a channel of blessing.

> Finally all of you be of one mind, having compassion for one another; love as brothers, be tenderhearted, be courteous; not returning evil for evil or reviling for reviling, but on the contrary blessing, knowing that you were called to this, that you may inherit a blessing   (1 Peter 3:8,9).

We are called by God to be blessings to others. We are to be of the same mind, have compassion for one another, love as brothers, be tenderhearted, courteous, and we are not to return evil for evil, insult for insult.

If we want to receive a blessing from God we must be blessings to others.

Interruptions may be the stepping stones to service. Inconveniences are God's testing points. We can discover significant things about ourselves. For instance, how willing are we to put aside our own wants and wishes?

The next time the phone rings and we are busily engrossed, let us pray that we will be *channels of blessing.*

When you answer the phone in the morning, I would suggest that you answer in a cheerful voice: "Good Morning!"

Let folks know you are glad they called!

Give people your time. We often are willing to give everything except our time. Writing a check, for instance, is a poor substitute for giving ourselves.

In order for any of us to cultivate the servant's spirit we must put some effort into it. It's hard work to serve. It tires us but, as we grow in Christ, we will find ourselves being renewed day by day.

> Therefore we do not lose heart. Even though our outward man is perishing, yet the inward man is being renewed, day by day (2 Corinthians 4:16).

When my strength seems to be waning, I go to that verse. God's Word refreshes us . . . we cannot help but serve. When God is placed first, others second and ourselves last, servanthood will result.

Through interruptions we will be "serving one another in love," even though we may be getting nothing accomplished for ourselves. Let us pray for a happy spirit which desires only to please Him and help others along the way. Let us never confuse "being poor in spirit" with "having a poor spirit." Let us remember our holy calling.

Encourage One Another

Encouragement is another way of showing compassionate love.

> Let us not give up meeting together, as some are in the habit of doing, but let us encourage one another — and all the more as you see the Day approaching (Hebrews 10:25). (NIV)

The root word for "encouragement" is the Greek word *paraklesis* which means "one who comes along side to help."

It is very similar to the Hebrew word "helpmeet" or "helper." One of the first titles God ever gave a woman was "helper." The Hebrew meaning is "one who assists another to reach complete fulfillment." It is used in other places in the Bible to refer to "someone who comes to rescue another."

It was also very interesting to discover that the Greek word *paraklesis* is similar to the word *paracletos* which is used to describe the Holy Spirit. The Holy Spirit is our advocate and comforter — our Helper. In John 14:16 we read: "And I will pray the Father, and He will give you another Helper, that He may abide with you forever."

An advocate is someone who is *for you*. A comforter soothes in distress and sorrow, easing the misery or grief. That's what our Holy Spirit does for us. We can imitate the Holy Spirit when we comfort or encourage another. "Encouragement is oxygen to the soul" someone has written.

A discouraged person is one who lacks courage, one who has lost heart. To encourage such a person is a true expression of love. Encouragement is another way to "inspire with courage."

I met "Miss Marie," an apple cheeked, lovely little lady with a twinkle in her eye at one of our seminars recently. The widow of a former elder, she was very modest about her present service in the family of God.

"Since my husband died," she said to me, "I don't feel like I do very much, so I just encourage people!"

Not do very much! There is nothing more needed in the world today, than people (especially older women) who will encourage and cheer other's hearts.

Few people (no matter how much spiritual fervor they have) will continue serving God unless someone gives them a pat on the back, a kind word, a recognition of a "job well done." There is always something we can say that will encourage them to "keep on keeping on."

We can help "bear one another's burdens" (their overload) by conscientiously encouraging another. Psalm 27:13 tells us:

> I would have lost heart
> unless I had believed
> That I would see the
> goodness of the Lord
> In the land of the living.

Any of us will lose heart without the goodness of the Lord. We also need the "goodness" of other people.

When our daughter Patty was at Harding University, I was impressed with her thoughtful acts of kindness to her friends. She was always encouraging her friends with notes and telephone calls. She would go out of her way to befriend unlovely people. One day while visiting in her room, I noticed this poem upon her wall:

> Be a blessing to someone today
> Share the light — throw the darkness away
> Let the Jesus in you
> Be the thing that shines through . . .
> Be a blessing to someone today.
>
>   — Author Unknown

We are told in Isaiah 42:3 and again in Matthew 12:20:

> A bruised reed He will not break,
> And smoking flax He will not quench.

This is speaking of the compassionate attitude our Lord had toward broken and bruised people. This is a picture which portrays the human condition as well. We do not need someone to come along and break us or to blow out our flickering candle. We need someone to *warm* us.

Ways to Encourage Our Husbands

Hebrews 10:24 tells us: "Let us consider how we may spur one another on toward love and good deeds..."

In context, this refers to encouraging one another in the body of Christ. How much more should we encourage and spur one another on within our marriages for we are one flesh.

There are many ways we as wives can encourage and comfort our husbands. One of the best ways is making him feel appreciated. Instead of complaining about our husband's shortcomings and criticizing him all the time, we can compliment him and make him feel needed and wanted.

We all hunger to be loved and we want tangible proof that we are loved. Robert Lewis Stevenson spoke the truth when he said:

> Here we are, most of us, sitting at the window of our heart, crying for someone to come in and love us. But then we cover up the window with the stained glass of pride or anger or self-pity, so that no one can glimpse the lonely self inside.

Here are a few "sweet" words we can shower upon our husbands, remembering "A word fitly spoken is like apples of gold in settings of silver" (Proverbs 25:11).

> I love you.
> You are my best friend. I like you too.
> I need you so much.
> I think you are the greatest.
> I think you are wonderful. (One husband said: "My wife keeps telling me that I'm the greatest husband in the world, and I know that I'm not

the best one — but I'm not going to argue with a woman as smart as my wife!")
You do that so well.
You are so much like Christ. I want to be like you.
You are so kind, so good, so thoughtful.
Thank you for being you.
Thank you for all the things you do for me.
You are so good with the children.
Thank you for being such a good father.
I wish I had said that!
Thank you for being such a good lover.
I wish I could be as smart as you.
I love the way that suit looks on *you*.
I love your smile, your hands, your arms around me.
I love how you pray ... how well you teach ...
I love the way you lead singing (or whatever he does best.)
I love the way you presented that sermon. You developed it so well.
Honey, you make me really think.
I love the way I can always count on you.
There's no one like you in the whole world.
Thank God ... He gave me you!

Yes, we as loving wives can be the stimulus to "spur our husbands on to love and good deeds."

A husband can go out into the world and do most anything if he has a wife who believes in him and who encourages him in good things.

The times we really bless and help our husbands are the times we drop everything to listen, watch, applaud and brag on our husband's achievements. I do not think I will ever gain the "women's lib" approval in these remarks, but I believe this is what God's Word tells us to do.

The Power of Love

Let us not be fearful in serving others. 2 Timothy 1:7 shows us why:

> For God has not given us the spirit of fear; but of power, and of love and of a sound mind.

If we have a spirit of fear, know one thing. God did not give it to us. He gives us the spirit of power, of love and a sound mind. Christ can do things through us we thought impossible. Christ came to live out His love life in us. Remember, others will know we are Christians by our love!

The Power of Love

Once there was a little piece of iron, which looked very frail but was really very strong. One after another had tried to break it but failed.

"I'll master it," said the ax; and his blows fell heavily on the iron.

But every blow made his edge more blunt until it ceased to strike.

"Leave it to me," said the saw and with his relentless teeth he worked backward and forward on its surface until they were all worn and broken, and he fell aside.
"Ha, Ha!" said the hammer. "I knew you wouldn't succeed, I'll show you the way."

But at the first fierce blow, off flew his head, and the iron remained as before.

"Shall I try?" asked the soft, small flame.

They all despised the flame; but he curled gently around the iron, embraced it, and never left it until it melted under his irresistible influence.

There are hearts hard enough to resist the force of wrath, the malice of persecution, and the fury of pride, but there is a power stronger than any of these. Hard indeed is the heart that can resist love.

— Author Unknown

We are to warm this old world with sparks of love and devotion. We are to serve as living blazers through which the love of God is kindled and inflamed.

In Summation

Someday we are going to stand before the great white throne of God. We are going to hear Him pronounce judgement on us. We all await with bated breath these wonderful words:

> Well done, good and faithful servant; you have been faithful over a few things, I will make you ruler over many things. Enter into the joy of your Lord (Matthew 25:23).

A Woman's Spirit of Service

If I were a man . . .
I would go to foreign lands
And "preach to all the nations."
I would deliver great messages of love
As a preacher to the local congregation.
I would lead prayers for the many
Full of faith and hope.

I would direct glorious singing
To you and your magnitude.
I would be the head of my household
And uphold your standards always.
These things I would do
If I were a man.

But Lord, you have not made me to be a man
You have made me to be a woman
And though many times
I long to do the things
That only men can do,
I know I have a place as a woman.

For as a woman . . .
I will exhibit Your spirit
Through my actions and attitudes.
I will help those who are needy
Both physically and spiritually.
I will deliver messages of love
To my fellow Christian women.

I will maintain a constant and meaningful
Prayer life with You.
I will assist my family
In upholding Your standards.

Lord, please give me a spirit of service.

— Shannon Caldwell

When a pebble or stone is dropped or thrown into a lake, immediately the quiet surface of the water is disturbed. One watches with wonder as ever-widening ripples circle on and on.
This is what happens when we cultivate the servant's spirit.

CHAPTER THIRTEEN

SOMETHING TO THINK ABOUT TODAY

1. Galatians 5:13 tells us to serve one another in _____.
2. Jesus told us how one could recognize a disciple. What is the criteria?
3. Describe the unconditional love of Jesus. How does it compare with our love?
4. What does the word "compassion" mean? Who was our greatest example?
5. Name seven ways the good Samaritan showed compassion.
6. In Luke 10:27 we are given the law of love and life. Put this Scripture on your refrigerator and meditate upon it for one week.
7. The reason why we do not love more _____ is because we do not love more _____.
8. Describe what deep love means?
9. One of the ways we can cultivate a loving compassionate spirit is by _____ _____ _____.
10. This is called the ministry of the _____ _____.
11. We are called by God to be _____ to others.
12. Explain what we mean by stating that inconveniences are God's testing points.
13. What would be a good way to answer the phone in the morning?
14. _____ is another way of showing compassionate love.
15. The root word for encouragement is _____ which means _____ _____ _____ _____ _____ _____ _____.
16. Name a few "sweet" ways we can encourage our husbands.
17. We are to warm this world with sparks of _____ and _____.
18. Repeat from memory the words of Matthew 25:23. Why do these words give us so much joy and hope?
19. What happens when a pebble or stone is thrown into a lake?
20. Why do you want to cultivate the servant's spirit?

CHURCH OF CHRIST, EAST FRAYSER
2285 FRAYSER BLVD.
MEMPHIS, TN 38127
(901) 357-7444